instinct

Also by Sherrilyn Kenyon

Illusion

Inferno

Infinity

Invincible

Infamous

The Dark-Hunters, Volume 1

The Dark-Hunters, Volume 2

The Dark-Hunters, Volume 3

The Dark-Hunters, Volume 4

CHRONICLES
of NICK

instinct

SHERRILYN KENYON

St. Martin's Griffin ⪯ *New York*

INSTINCT. Copyright © 2015 by Sherrilyn Kenyon. All rights reserved. Printed in the United States of America. For information, address St. Martin's Press, 175 Fifth Avenue, New York, N.Y. 10010.

www.stmartins.com

The Library of Congress has cataloged the hardcover edition as follows:

Kenyon, Sherrilyn, 1965–
    Instinct / Sherrilyn Kenyon. — First edition.
        p. cm. — (Chronicles of Nick ; [6])
    ISBN 978-1-250-06386-1 (hardcover)
    ISBN 978-1-4668-6886-1 (e-book)
    [1. Supernatural—Fiction. 2. High schools—Fiction. 3. Schools—Fiction. 4. New Orleans (La.)—Fiction.] I. Title.
    PZ7.K432Ins 2015
    [Fic]—dc23

                                                          2015001980

ISBN 978-1-250-06387-8 (trade paperback)

Our books may be purchased in bulk for promotional, educational, or business use. Please contact your local bookseller or the Macmillan Corporate and Premium Sales Department at (800) 221-7945, extension 5442, or by e-mail at MacmillanSpecialMarkets@macmillan.com.

First St. Martin's Griffin Trade Paperback Edition: May 2016

10 9 8 7 6 5 4 3

In loving memory of Fred Grimm, whose last name was the biggest misnomer of all. Nick proudly dons his bright Hawaiian shirts in your honor, my brother. You are and will always be missed.

To Stephania, for being another bright and shining light in this world. God bless and keep you always, my sister. I love you dearly! And I think of you every day.

For Mama Lisa, Greg, and Sister Kim, for keeping me sane and for reasons y'all know. I couldn't have done it without you! And for Judy, Loretta, Paco, Carl and Jacs and Pam and my two nurse Kims! And always Red Kim. :)

Last, but never, ever least, my husband and boys, for inspiring me and putting up with my most forgetful ways and long, solitary hours of writing time. I couldn't make it through my days or life without you.

And to my awesome agent and team at SMP, and especially my wonderful editor, who hasn't used her voodoo doll on me yet. Thank you! I'm so blessed to have all of you in my life and I'm so glad all of you are part of my world!

A good friend once told me not to dread the future. One way or another, it would come. The trick was to meet it with open arms so that when it ran me over, it wouldn't break anything.

—*Renegade Waya Mayan Dark-Hunter*

instinct

PROLOGUE

It wasn't easy being Death. Made it hard to make friends. Harder still to keep them. No one was ever really happy to see you. Being around anyone tended to make them nervous and jumpy. Really sucked most days.

And today in particular, Grim was . . . well . . . Grim.

Sighing heavily, he glared at his hulking henchmen, Pain and Suffering. Instantly terrified of Grim's intent and mood and what it might cause him to do to them, they skittered from the room like two roaches caught trying to pilfer a bite of cake. As if he was going to kill them while they were cleaning his office.

Later, he might be tempted. But he seldom killed anyone while they were doing something *for* him.

Even more agitated by their fear, he skimmed his hand over the large crystal skull on his table. Time was being tampered with. He didn't know why and he didn't know who.

But something wasn't right. Something unnatural was happening. And this stupid, clear skull wasn't helping him decipher the riddle in the least. He saw nothing, and that only ticked him off more. He'd never liked being in the dark. Never liked not knowing, and he cursed the day he'd been born without foresight.

Grim lifted the skull up, intending to splinter it against the wall.

"Are you trying to find our missing rider?"

Calming enough to return the skull to its stand, Grim cocked his head at the sound of the feminine voice. With long, curly dark hair and perfect features, Laguerre was ever beautiful. Ever evil. His favorite kind of being, if the truth were told. There was no ambiguity in her heart. No prejudice. She hated everyone equally.

And she killed without hesitation.

It was why they were best friends and had been so for countless centuries. Sighing in the midst of his bitter ennui, Grim sat back in his chair to eye her ruefully. "There's no reason to hunt for Yrre. Sadly, Gautier refused the call and closed the door on our ride against the human vermin. There's nothing we can do now."

"Yes, but he left all the riders on the human side of it when he so rudely slammed it shut in our faces. *None* of us are trapped in other realms this time."

She had a point. Still . . .

"Bane is aligning himself with our enemies. He says he's done with the intrigue. It's just you and me now."

"And Yrre, with one more who is willing and bitter enough to join us. One who has the blood and fury we need to pull the ancient gods into this world and unleash them. They will be forever grateful for our service and they will reward our loyalty. While four is not as strong as our seven, four riders make a formidable team . . . and the majority we need to call for a judgment and take back what was stolen from us."

Grim quirked a brow at that. "Pardon?"

"I found our missing rider who's more than willing to eat the heart of the Malachai and lead us to Conquest. Together, we can make our Malachai-Gautier demon all he should be. Or kill him if he refuses and replace him with his brother, the elder child who bears Malachai blood."

For the first time since Nick Gautier had fought his way back to the right dimension and decided not to end the world or die in utter agony at his feet, Grim smiled.

Things were finally looking up again. And this time, nothing would stop them. Especially not some smart-mouthed guttersnipe teenager and his motley band of friends. And little Nick was about to learn just what a liability friends really were.

CHAPTER 1

✻

Nickaboo? Hurry, child! You're about to be late for school!"

Nick Gautier dropped the towel from the damp hair he was drying as he glanced to the clock on his nightstand to confirm the fact that his mother was still the most vigilant and accurate timekeeper in the history of all mankind. At least when it came to his home, school, and work schedules.

But how odd . . . he'd had almost forty minutes just a heartbeat ago when he'd left the bathroom.

How long did it take to pull on a pair of jeans and one really foully ugly Hawaiian shirt, anyway?

Apparently thirty-five minutes.

Dang, I do move slow in the morning. Good thing his mortal enemies didn't know that. He'd be Cajun hashbrowns.

Tossing the towel into the bathroom, he rushed to the kitchen and almost tripped over their newest furry addition.

Xevikan, who let out a nasty hiss in protest before he scurried to the corner to arch his back against the wall.

Nick started to return the cat's growl, but since his mom didn't know their new pet was actually a shape-shifting ancient Nick and his friends had freed from a hell dimension and taken in, he refrained. His luck, she'd think *he* had distemper or something, and take him in for shots. "Sorry, Mr. Fuzzy Boots."

Xev glared at him before he mentally projected his ire at him. *I really hate that name you gave my feline incarnation, Gautier.*

Nick flashed a grin at the large white Egyptian Mau staring up at him indignantly. *Why you think I use it?*

Xev spread his claws for cleaning, but Nick caught the one he aimed directly at him.

Laughing good-naturedly at the single-finger insult Xev had picked up from Caleb, Nick started to reach for the bacon only to realize his furry houseguest had beat him to it. Again. Yeah, it was a good thing he felt sorry for Xev.

And he did. For thousands of years, the ancient being had been imprisoned in a realm without friend or family. Now Xev was extremely gun-shy of a world he didn't understand, nor did he play well with others, which was why they'd decided the best thing was to leave him here in Nick's house to sleep while Nick went to school and work. All of them were much happier that way. And since Xev had severe PTSD mixed with extremely frightening powers and not a lot of patience or tolerance, the world was a lot less likely to end violently if Xev stayed out of events that elevated his stress levels, and tempted him to mass homicide.

"Really, Nick? Really?"

He turned to find his petite, blond mother glaring up at him. Man, he'd never understand how a woman as tiny as Cherise Gautier could be so terrifying when riled. But then, his girlfriend, Nekoda Kennedy, had those same testosterone-sucking powers, too.

And all Kody had to do to wield hers was pout in his general direction.

"What?"

Closing the fridge door, his mom wiggled the milk container at him. "First, why did you drink all the milk last night *after* I went to bed? Second, why did you put the empty container *back* in the fridge?"

He clamped his jaw shut and slid his gaze to the real culprit, who'd probably drunk out of the container without a glass on top of it all. But his mom would think him nuts if he blamed the empty milk jug on the cat lacking opposable thumbs. So he manned up and took the fall for his friend.

"Blatant stupidity? I find it to be responsible for the vast majority of evil I unintentionally do."

She rolled her eyes and tossed the milk carton into the garbage. "Go on before you get another tardy. Love you, even when you make me crazy."

"You, too." He grabbed his backpack from the

floor, kissed her cheek, and glared at the cat. "Later, Fuzzy Boots." *And don't defile my bedsheets!*

It was too late. Xev was already beelining to Nick's room to take his shift in the bed.

Sighing at the uselessness of warning Xev off anything, Nick glanced back at his mom. "I'll grab more milk on my way home from work."

"Thank you, Boo. Have a good day."

"You, too. Don't work too hard." Nick headed out the back door and crossed the condo parking lot to the brick wall that separated it from the school yard. Even though there were storm clouds gathering in the distance, and headed in from over the river, he took a moment to appreciate the day.

Zipping his jacket, he inhaled the familiar smell of beignets and coffee that wafted on the breeze, coming in from the Market and restaurants. Honestly, he was grateful to be home in the French Quarter, and among his friends and family.

To be standing here, in the most beautiful city in all the world.

Yeah, it was a good day to be alive. His friend, Acheron, who was an ancient Atlantean, was right, every day should be met with purpose and lived with gratitude. Having been forced against his will to live as someone else for a brief time, Nick had decided that as screwed up and dangerous as his real life was, he much preferred it to anyone else's.

This existence and world might not be perfect. But they were perfectly his. The only thing he'd change at this point was the number of paranormal creatures who wanted him dead.

Or enslaved.

Yeah, it would be nice to be off a few hit lists for a while. *That* he wouldn't complain about.

Eh, ca c'est bon. That was life. Some days you ate the *rougarou*. Some days the *rougarou* devoured you.

And in this city, and in his particularly screwed-up life, that phrase seriously had significance.

Sprinting up the steps of St. Richard's High School, he entered the two-story redbrick building and headed for his locker to change out his books so he could start his day right, and with as little drama as possible. Which would be a really nice change of pace.

"What are you smiling about, Gautier?"

Nick grinned even wider as he shut his locker and turned to face his recalcitrant demon bodyguard. "It's almost 8 A.M. and nothing's tried to kill or eat me yet. Dang good day, if you ask me."

Rolling his eyes, Caleb stepped around him to open his own locker. "I really hate chipper morning people. Thinking I should have hand-fed you to your enemies last night."

Nick laughed. "But you didn't," he teased against all common sense, in a singsongy voice he'd learned from a very special Charonte demon named Simi, while Caleb pulled books out and shoved them into his expensive designer backpack. "Which means you think I'm all cute and fluffy. Besides, you'd miss me if I were gone."

With a rude snort, Caleb zipped his bag shut. "Careful, Cajun. I wouldn't test that theory, were I you."

Nick leaned up against the locker bank and tried not to envy Caleb his dark, perfect Hollywood good looks that made every female in their school pass a longing gaze at him as she walked by. Student and teacher. "That would hold more weight if you weren't here."

"Meaning?"

"You said if my demonic overlord of a father were dead, you wouldn't be in high school anymore to guard me. Now he's gone, and yet here you remain . . . ever my faithful, handsome protector." He batted his eyelashes playfully.

Ignoring Nick's feigned flirtations, Caleb shut the locker and brushed his hand through his stylishly coiffed jet-black hair. His dark eyes flashing orange, he gave Nick a harsh, unamused stare. "Yeah, well, my self-preservation and common sense kicked in. If something eats you, they inherit my servitude and soul. As annoying as you are most days, I'd rather deal with you than one of my other possible choices. 'Cause let's face it, my luck and past experiences say it would never be a sexy succubus who spends her days working as a supermodel in a bikini, but rather some scaly elderly male exhibitionist who likes to pull the wings off daeves and stick us in jars . . . or nail us to walls."

He shoved a chemistry book at Nick. "Been there. Done that. Reloop's a bitch and whoever designed it should be relegated to the lowest level of Thorn's special pit."

Nick tsked at him. "Poor Caleb. Thousands of years old and still in high school. Dude, you seriously need to speak to a guidance counselor about your transcript."

"Don't push it, Gautier. My maternal instincts don't kick in till noon."

Laughing, Nick stepped away from the lockers so that LaShonda could open hers. Dressed in a J-pop-style navy suit, she had her newly done sisterlocks pulled back into a matching bow.

"Morning, Miss Sunshine."

LaShonda scowled at him as she pulled books for her first period. "Someone's in a good mood this morning."

Nick winked at her. "What can I say? The sight of your beautiful face can cheer my most soured mood."

"Better not let her boyfriend or your Kody hear you speaking to her like that, Gautier, or they'll be having a pair of fried Cajun nuggets for lunch."

Smiling, Nick stepped aside for Brynna Addams, LaShonda's best friend, and one of the few people he knew he could count on whenever it mattered. Unlike LaShonda, with her daring style, Brynna was much more sedate in her wardrobe choice, with tan pants and a white shirt. "Morning, my other Miss Sunshine. Ever a pleasure to see you."

"You *are* in a good mood." Brynna started to scowl until her gaze went past him. By the shift in the air, his instincts told him someone with the highest level of supernatural abilities approached him from behind. Someone who was lethal and could kill him in a heartbeat. And without looking, he knew exactly who it was. A gifted celestial being whose qualities he was more than well acquainted with.

His heart even lighter, he turned and, blatantly ignoring the PDA laws of his school, wrapped his arms around Nekoda so that he could breathe in the light vanilla scent that was uniquely hers. Her brown hair was twisted up into a messy braid that framed a beautiful face. A face that held a pair of bright green eyes that never failed to set his blood on fire. Even though she'd originally been sent here to assassinate him before he fulfilled his prophecy of doom, and Caleb still had his doubts about trusting her loyalty to them, Nick couldn't help his feelings for her.

She was his first love.

Honestly, he couldn't imagine ever feeling like this about anyone else. And if he had to die, he'd rather it be by her hand than that of an enemy. His heart would always be hers, and no one else's.

He gave her a tight squeeze. "And here's the brightest part of any day. Good morning, *cher*."

With a fierce frown, Nekoda brushed the dark hair back from his face. "You okay?"

Brynna smirked as she opened her locker. "Girl, he's in a strange, strange mood. I'm wondering if Madaug's been programming games again."

Nekoda laughed nervously at the reminder of the Zombie Hunter game Madaug St. James had created that had accidentally turned half their football team into mindless zombies and caused their former coach to eat their previous principal.

"He hasn't, has he?"

"No. Definitely not. He hasn't even played Solitaire on his PC since that night." Nick took Kody's backpack from her hand so that he could carry it for her. "I'm alive. In New Orleans, where I'm supposed to be. Here with you, the most beautiful girl in the entire universe." He kissed her cheek before he jerked his chin toward Caleb. "And we have King Grump scowling at us and plotting my death and dismemberment. All is right in this world. And I'm just really glad to be at this school, in this time where I belong, with all of you thinking I've lost my ever-loving mind."

Caleb scoffed. "For the love of all that's holy, would you stop saying that crap?" he ground out between clenched teeth. "Personally, I wouldn't tempt the Fates, kid. They have a nasty way of ramming those pleasant thoughts down your throat and making you weep for them."

Nick considered that for a moment. Then, closing the distance between him and Caleb, he couldn't resist whispering the question that comment most begged for, "In a fight between the Malachai demon and the Fates, who would win?"

Placing a hand on Nick's shoulder, Caleb gently shoved him back. "Beware of arrogance, Gautier. It's a foul, fatal thing."

"I was only postulating a question."

The look on Caleb's face was intense and chilling. "Pray you never find out the answer. The price of war is always a lot higher in the end than you think it will be when you go in for that first battle."

Okay then . . .

Suddenly, a shiver went down Nick's spine. Something he couldn't quite identify. For a moment, he wasn't in the hallway of his high school.

Rather, Nick stared down at himself as he stood inside the ruins of a Greek temple. A temple he remembered visiting one time before when he'd saved Nekoda's life after she'd almost died in an attack on him.

Home of the enigmatic Artemis, goddess of the hunt.

Only the Greek goddess wasn't here this time. He

knew without being told that this was another glimpse of the horrific future to come.

The post-Apocalyptic future where he destroyed everything and everyone. Where he and his army laid waste to the entire world.

All of Olympus was on fire around him, and each temple had been leveled. Nick, in his true demonic form with black and red marbled skin and glowing eyes, stood defiant and strong, his wings tucked in at his back. His army hovered nearby, awaiting more orders from him. Blood from the ancient gods dripped from their armor.

And his.

Time slowed down as he watched himself searching the ruins, looking for something he seemed to have lost.

All sound stopped. He only heard his heartbeat. Fierce. Strong.

Defiant.

Ambrose . . .

He flinched at the unfamiliar voice in his head.

Well, crap. Unknown voices in his head was never a good sign. Especially when they wanted his undivided attention and used a name they weren't supposed to know.

And as fast as it started, it ended.

Like a sped-up video file, everything around him caught up to real time. He was back at his school, in his hallway with Caleb, Brynna, Kody, and LaShonda staring at him.

"Nick?"

He opened his mouth to respond to Kody and couldn't. Again, he had that frightening surreal feeling as everything in the hallway slowed down to a crawl.

Suddenly, he heard the strange eerie drumming of hooves rushing toward him. The sound of a horse screeching. It drowned out all other high school noises. Against his will, Nick turned in the hallway to see a rider in white billowing robes racing down the north hall on the back of a black horse as it passed through students and faculty. Snorting fire, the horse had blood-red eyes, searing with their hatred.

The rider held a set of old-fashioned scales in its hands. "Ambrose!" The voice was neither male nor female. It was strictly demonic and cold. Terrifying. Without pausing, it came straight at him in a dead run.

Unable to move, Nick was frozen as horse and rider tore through him and left him completely breathless and cold.

"Nick!"

Blinking at Kody, he shook his head to clear his vision as the main doors were blown open by the rider only he could see. Not even Kody or Caleb had detected it. They stared at him with duplicate frowns as teachers rushed to close the doors they thought the wind had caught.

How was *that* possible? They always saw things like that when he did. Usually *before* he did.

He opened his mouth to answer Kody at the same time the bell rang. *What the . . . ?*

Nick blinked as he glanced around at everyone in the hallway. They were now all scrambling to get to their rooms. He'd had fifteen minutes until class a heartbeat ago.

Hadn't he?

He glanced to the hall clock that confirmed it was time for school to start. *That can't be right.*

"Gautier?" Caleb barked from the door of their homeroom. How had he gotten there so fast? Surely he hadn't teleported in front of the humans. "You shooting for another tardy?"

A big negatory on that. He spent enough of his teenhood in this building. Last thing he wanted was to donate any additional time to it, especially when he didn't have to. Shrugging off his delusions that he attributed to some kind of weird Nintendo-induced flashback, Nick headed into the room where Nekoda, Brynna, and Caleb were taking their seats.

Still, something seemed off. Like he was walking through heavy, thick foam . . . He leaned over to whisper to Nekoda. "I'm where I'm supposed to be, right?"

Her scowl matched his. "Are you my Nick?"

God, he hoped so. Why else would he be dressed in this fugly orange trout Hawaiian shirt? Last time he'd been in another dimension and body, he'd had a much better wardrobe. He'd also been a lot shorter than his normal, gangly, six-foot-four, bang-my-knees-into-everything stature.

He hesitated. "Are you *my* Kody?" he asked her.

"Yes," she dragged the answer out. "Why are you asking?"

Nick rubbed at his neck. "Don't know. Got a weird feeling all of a sudden."

"It's called detention, Mr. Gautier." Richardson ripped off the paper with times and a room number for said punishment, and set it on the desk in front of him. "See you after school."

Epically awesome.

Nick wasn't sure what ticked him off more. The detention or the fact that the troll still couldn't pronounce his name right. She always said "Gah-tee-ay" when she knew it was Cajun and pronounced "Go-shay."

Don't say a word.

He grimaced at Caleb's voice in his head. Normally, he wouldn't have listened. But for once, he was too grateful that this was typical of his luck, and deci-

ded to heed Caleb's good advice. No need to antago-
nize the establishment.

Today, anyway. He just wanted the rest of the day
to settle down and return to normal. No more freaky
ghosts in the hall. No more unknown voices in his
head.

Normal.

*Please, for the love of God, let my day be normal for
once. . . .*

"What?" Richardson snarled. "No smart retort,
Mr. Gautier? Cat swallow your tongue?"

Nick gave her a charming grin he didn't really feel.
"No, ma'am. A gator named Sense Formerly Known
as Common."

Sneering at him, she tottered her way to her desk
so that she could insult someone else and ruin *their* day.

Caleb let out an annoyed breath. *Great,* he projected to Nick. *Now I have to get detention, too. I really
hate you, Gautier.*

Nick batted his eyelashes at Caleb. *But I wubs you,
Caliboo.*

That succeeded in wringing a groan out of Caleb.

"What was that, Mr. Malphas?" Richardson asked.

"Severe intestinal woe caused by an external hemorrhoid that seems to be growing on my right-hand side." He cast a meaningful glower toward Nick.

The class erupted into laughter as Richardson shot to her feet. "Enough!" She slammed her hands on her desk. "For that, Mr. Malphas, you can join Mr. Gautier in after-school detention."

Caleb let out an irritated sigh. *More quality time with my hemorrhoid. Just what I wanted for Christmas. Yippee ki-yay.*

Nick forced himself not to react to the sarcastic words only he could hear. If not for the fact that he knew the truth behind Caleb's feelings where he was concerned, he'd be hurt by that animosity. But while he'd been trapped out of his body in another dimension, he'd seen and heard firsthand what Caleb really thought about him.

They were family.

Brothers in arms.

Yes, they fought and sniped. Yet at the end of the

day, they would kill or die for each other. It was something each of them had proven. Of that, he had no doubt.

So he took the acerbic demon in stride and tried to keep in mind how hard life had to be for Caleb. He'd lost everyone he cared about. Had seen his wife brutally slain by his enemies and had spent centuries enslaved to a cruel, demonic master who'd hated his guts. One who hadn't hesitated to abuse and mock him every chance he could. Yeah, Nick's father had been a rank dog to everyone around him. Caleb had every reason in the universe to hate Nick, and instead, he was the best friend Nick had ever known.

Hey, bud, Nick mentally projected to Caleb. *Thanks.*

Caleb scowled. "For?"

Nick smiled as Caleb spoke out loud. *Not letting me die. Fighting by my side whenever I need you to, and for getting up this morning when I know you'd rather sleep till noon or later.*

His frown deepened. *You're so weird.*

Given the fact that Nick was the hated son of a demon whose sole purpose was to one day end the world—and had been born the lead rider of the Apocalypse, Conquest, to be specific, and he was currently dating the ghost of a warrior he would kill in their future—*weird* was a massive understatement.

For that matter, if there was a primer for normality, Nick would be the first in line to buy it. His life was ever a case study of Murphy's Law to the utter extremes.

Whatever can go wrong, will go wrong. And in the worst way possible, at the worst possible time.

Yeah, that summed up his average day. Sad thing was, he was getting really used to that.

Just as the bell rang, Caleb sneezed.

Then sneezed again. And once more.

Nick froze at the startling sound he'd never heard before. Ever. Especially given the fact that Caleb's features instantly paled.

"You all right, buddy?"

Caleb brushed his hand against his brow in a way that said it was not a good day to be Malphas. "I don't feel well all of a sudden."

"You don't look so good either."

"Sheez, Nick! You're so blunt!" Kody chided as she

stepped around him to check on Caleb. She placed her hand on Caleb's forehead. "Gracious, hon. You're burning with a fever."

Caleb shook his head. "No. Can't be. I don't get sick." He started coughing. Hard.

Wide-eyed, Nick stepped back. "While I'm no medic or nurse, that sounds pretty sick to me. And not the good kind of sick. The sick kind of sick. Like call-my-mama-I-need-soup-and-Kleenex sick."

Kody patted Caleb on the back. "You okay, sweetie?"

Nodding, he drew a ragged breath. Then he started coughing again.

Richardson came over to them with an irritated sneer. "Is there a problem?"

Nick exchanged a worried glance with Kody before he answered. "I think Caleb's illin'."

Scoffing, Richardson curled her lip. "He looks fine to—"

Her words broke off as Caleb hurled at her feet. Shrieking, she jumped back, but not before he scored on her ugly brown ortho shoes.

Nick wrinkled his nose. "Dude, that's so gross!"

But awesome as all get-out! Nice to know Caleb had great aim in all things. "Man, what'd you eat for breakfast? That don't look right. Is that small kitten bits or something?"

Turning bright green herself and retching, Richardson cursed them in a way that would have them suspended if the principal overheard one of them say that. "Take him to the office. Now!"

"Yes, ma'am." Nick pressed his lips together to keep from laughing over the nasty retribution as he pulled Caleb's arm around his shoulders and led him toward the front of school. Kody followed behind them.

As soon as they were clear of the room, Nick paused to whisper. "You want me to take you to the bathroom so you can teleport home?"

Caleb wheezed. "I-I-I can't teleport."

Nick went cold with dread. "What?"

Stark cold terror filled Caleb's dark eyes. "My powers are gone, Nick. I'm human."

CHAPTER 2

Nick opened his mouth to tell Caleb he wasn't funny, but before he could, Caleb dashed into the bathroom and to a stall to be sick again. Thankfully, he didn't score on Nick before he left.

Or his shoes.

Bonus for that. Though, to be honest, if Caleb had taken out the hideous shirt, Nick wouldn't have complained too much.

Cringing at the sounds of gastro-misery coming out of his friend, Nick waited by the sinks until Caleb was through. Pale and shaking, Caleb stumbled out a few minutes later. Man, he felt bad for the demon.

Nick turned the water on for him and stood aside while Caleb washed up. "You gonna make it?"

Before Caleb could answer, his knees buckled.

Seriously concerned, Nick caught him up against his side. "Caleb?" Kody was right. He was burning with a fever so severe, it radiated through his clothes. "Can you hear me?"

He started babbling in demonkyn. Something about fields and planting? It was so off and made no sense whatsoever. Why would a daeve warrior demon care about planting a field?

"Caleb!" Nick barked. "Dude! I need you to hang with me. C'mon. Don't do this. I need you lucid."

It was useless. Caleb had checked out and taken the bill with him.

Had the ghost rider in the hallway caused this? It didn't seem possible, but what else could have done it? He'd been fine earlier.

Biting his lip, Nick debated what to do. Who to go to for help.

One thing was clear. No one else in their school needed to know about this. Nor did they need to witness Caleb speaking in tongues. They might start asking awkward questions about what language it was. Why Caleb knew it.

Or worse, they could discover Caleb's *and* Nick's less-than-human origins. While most of their private parochial school was human, there were enough preternaturals here to make it real uncomfortable for Nick's small group. Especially when it came to the staff clergy, who might want them exorcized.

Or worse . . .

Expelled.

For that matter, while there were humans here who knew about and protected the other preters at the school, none of them were aware that they had a small demon population, and they really wanted to keep it that way.

The fewer who knew about Nick and Caleb, the better. Since most people assumed every species of demon was evil and all they wanted was to throw holy water on them and banish them straight to hell, no good could come of anyone knowing about them. The last thing Nick wanted was that kind of negative attention and stereotyping. He had a hard enough time with puberty and dating. No need to toss *this* into the mix, too, and have Sister Katherine following them around with her rosary and thurible.

As with humanity, demons came in all breeds and kinds, and they chose which side of the fight they wanted to be on. For now, he and Caleb were firmly rooted on the right side, and they both planned to stay here no matter what.

But because people had a nasty tendency to attack without question, they wouldn't believe that about them. He accepted and respected the fact that demons had a bad rep. Most had earned it, yet Nick didn't want to be judged by those who'd come before him.

He was here to make his own way in this world. And he would be saved or condemned by the choices he, alone, made. Not for the deeds of others.

Yet that was neither here nor there. Right now, his main concern was what to do for Caleb. How best to protect and help his friend.

Nick glanced around to make sure no one else was

in the bathroom with them before he flashed them to Caleb's house. It was the only safe place he could take Caleb to heal where neither his nor Caleb's enemies could get to him.

"Zavid!"

The Aamon demon who lived with Caleb, Zavid, appeared at his side immediately, then stepped back as soon as he saw Caleb's weakened condition, and heard his babbling. Like Caleb, Zavid had dark hair and the kind of build and good looks that left Nick feeling without. "What did you do to him, Malachai?"

"Nothing. He got sick."

That didn't help Zavid's attitude toward Nick. If anything, he only became more suspicious. "We don't get sick."

Caleb began coughing up blood, maybe even a kidney from the sounds of it, as he staggered away. He only made it as far as the stairs before he sat down and leaned against the wall.

Nick cringed at how awful his friend looked. Those were deep, bronchial coughs like Nick used to get when he was a kid. He had no idea what to do for him. He seriously doubted an inhaler would help. "I feel like I ought to make you chicken soup or something."

His breathing labored, Caleb stared at him. "How does anyone stand this?"

"Usually? With a great deal of whining and begging for my mom to come baby me."

Zavid scowled. "This isn't a joke? He really is sick?"

"Yeah."

Zavid glanced from Nick to Caleb and back again. "Not injured? Sick?"

"Sick," Nick repeated.

Arms akimbo, Zavid stood in a state of utter disbelief as Caleb sat on the stairs with his head in his hands. "How is this possible?"

"No idea. Isn't there a demon doctor or something I can take him to? What do you guys do when you get ill?"

"We. Don't. Get. Sick." Zavid enunciated each word slowly. "Ever. We get injured. We get ticked off. We get dead. We *never* get sick."

Nick gestured at Caleb. "Obviously, you've been misinformed."

Zavid rolled his eyes. "Liv!" he barked, which, given the fact he was a Hel hound in his other form, meant something.

Dressed in a white flowing nightgown and with long black hair, Livia appeared instantly by Zavid's side. Unbelievably beautiful, she was also a demon general who was even more bloodthirsty than the guys. It made Nick glad that she was on their side.

Yawning, she rubbed at her eyes. Obviously, she'd been sound asleep when he shouted for her. "What?" she said irritably.

"Ever heard of a demon getting sick?" Zavid asked.

She pursed her lips. "Of humans? All the time. It's what we live for."

Zavid laughed. "No. Catching a cold."

"Oh . . ." Yawning again, she rubbed at her head. "Don't be stupid. Demons are immune from germs."

"And we're back where we started. Beginning to feel like I'm riding a hamster wheel." Nick jumped away as Caleb began a gurgling sound like he'd made right before he'd trashed Richardson's shoes. "I should probably mention that C doesn't have his powers, so one of you might want to get him a little closer to a bathroom. Just in case he starts blowing another gasket."

Zavid turned his attention to Livia.

Livia gaped at Zavid, then Nick. "What? 'Cause I'm female I'm the wet nurse?"

"Well, yeah . . . you have the anatomy for it we lack," Zavid said snidely.

Nick shrugged. "Don't look at me for this. As stated, I lack the necessary female equipment for wet nursery. And I once killed a cactus and Bubba's goldfish watching over them. No offense, I don't want to kill Malphas or find a toilet big enough to flush him down. Not even sure how to water him or what to feed him. Come to think of it, I don't recall him eating anything around me. Ever. Last time he went down, he told me he wanted blood to heal, and I only do that for the Red Cross."

Caleb looked up to curl his lip at Nick, but didn't comment on that. "Can someone please get me to bed?

I don't think I can make it up the stairs. And you should be grateful, Gautier. If I had the energy to stand, I'd probably strangle you. Or take an involuntary blood donation from your jugular."

He vanished instantly.

Zavid walked over to Nick. "I sent him to his bed. But really, what's going on? How can Malphas be sick and without his powers?"

"I don't know. Is there some kind of demon that preys on us?"

"Many," they said in unison.

Nick groaned. "Great. Good to know." Caleb had been right. He should have never said the day was going good. Everything had just skidded off the Crap Exit ramp into Hexville.

"But," Zavid interrupted his mental anguish, "never heard of anything like this." He glanced to Livia. "You?"

She shook her head. "Not with a demon as powerful and old as Malphas. If they had that kind of ability to strip *his* powers, they'd have attacked the Malachai before him."

"Yeah, but for once, nothing hit me."

Caleb let out an eerie, pain-filled howl. Terrified some new enemy was trying to kill or eat his best friend, Nick bolted up the stairs and into the bedroom to find Caleb motionless on the black sheets.

His heart stopped. Caleb looked so dead. His normally dark olive complexion had a bluish-gray cast to it.

Please. Please, don't have died. He really wasn't ready to say good-bye to his friend.

Not like this.

Nick approached the bed slowly and cautiously. There was no telling what could be going on. Terrified, he reached his hand out to check Caleb's breathing. It was faint, but it was still there.

Overwhelmed with relief, Nick sank to his knees by the bed and whispered a grateful prayer. "Hang in there, buddy. I'm going to find an answer for this. And get you right back on your feet. I promise."

He had no idea how, but there had to be some way to cure it. Some way to restore Caleb. It had to be a spell or curse or rabid dog hair, or something odd that was causing this. And if it was, then it could be undone.

Rising, he returned to Livia and Zavid, who waited at the bedroom door. "Watch him and make sure nothing else happens to him."

Zavid caught Nick's arm. "Where are you going?"

"To find a cure."

"And if you can't?" Livia asked.

Nick glanced back at Caleb and in his mind he saw the future where he lost everyone he loved. Saw himself standing alone, surrounded by flames and destruction. It was a future he refused to embrace.

His genetics, family, and birth would never define his fate. Only *he* would control his destiny. Not the gods and not some bullshit prophecy.

He met Livia's gaze and answered her question with every bit of Cajun stubbornness he possessed. "I will save him from this. Whatever it takes. Caleb has fought too many battles for me for me to turn my back on him now."

Zavid inclined his head respectfully to Nick. "I'll guard him with everything I have."

"Thanks. I'll be back as soon as I can."

Determined, Nick returned to school. He left the bathroom to find Kody still waiting for him in the hallway.

She glanced around Nick's shoulder, to the door. Then scowled. "Did you leave him in there?"

"Flashed him home."

She let out a relieved breath. "How's he doing?"

"Not good. He's in a coma or something."

Gaping in disbelief, she paled. "What? How is that possible?"

Nick shrugged. "I don't know. What do we do, Kody? I don't even have a clue on how to start to make him better."

"Me neither. I've never heard of this. What did Zavid and Liv say?"

"Demons don't get sick."

"They're right."

Nick glanced to the door where the rider had vanished before homeroom. "Did you see or feel anything earlier?"

"What do you mean?"

"Before class started? When you were trying to get my attention? I saw a rider on a black horse with scales come tearing down the hallway. He rode straight through me and out the door that was flung open for no reason."

She arched a brow at what he was saying. "Yrre? You saw Yrre? Here in the hallway?"

He shrugged. "I guess. Was that Yrre?"

"Dressed all in white?"

"Yeah."

She nodded slowly. "But Yrre isn't a guy. It's a woman."

"Oh. I didn't get that. I couldn't see a face or body shape. All I saw was the horse and the robes and scales. . . . You think she had something to do with this?"

Kody took a minute to consider that before she answered. "You and Caleb closed the gate, right? You sealed everything?"

"Caleb said we did."

"Then there's no way Yrre could be free. The ušumgallu can't assemble and ride without the

Malachai to lead them. You're their head and they need your blood to rise. . . . I think it must have been another of your visions. It's probably why you didn't know she was a woman and couldn't see her face. Maybe she was trying to reach out to you to get you to free her?"

That made sense, then. And she was right. In the past, Nick had always seen the riders in their true forms. Bane, Laguerre, and he was on first-name basis with Grim. They had come up to him as flesh-and-blood beings, not as the Ghost Rider of St. Richard's Before the Bell.

But something was attacking Caleb. Something that was out to harm them all.

"You think it might be a sickness the Arelim sent to weaken him and get back at me?" An ancient society of divine protectors for humans, the Arelim were charged with maintaining order and ensuring that the Malachai demon remained dormant. Unfortunately, some of them had decided the best way to do that was to kill off Nick before he came into his full Malachai powers. They were the ones who'd originally resurrected Nekoda after her death in a future battle, and had sent her back in time to kill him before he matured.

Now that he had inherited his father's powers, they wanted him dead before he mastered any more of them. And because Kody had blatantly refused to carry out her assassination orders, she wasn't on good terms with them anymore, either.

Their rebel sect wanted her dead as much as they did him.

Kody shook her head. "If they were able to do that to Caleb, they'd have gone after you instead."

Everything kept coming back to that one basic oh-so-testicle-shriveling fact. While the Arelim were in the middle of a bloody civil war, Nick was the number-one target for the rebels. They'd give anything to lay hands to him.

Kody was right. If they had something powerful enough to take down Caleb, they wouldn't have wasted it on Nick's protector.

They'd have unleashed it on Nick and taken his head as their trophy.

"This day just couldn't get any stranger." No sooner

had those words left his lips than the lights went out in the school and the building shook as a loud clap of thunder sounded right before hail pelted down.

Hard.

"Nick . . . you've got to quit saying such things."

"Yeah. If—"

Kody covered his mouth with her hands before he could speak another word. "I'm not kidding. You are one of the handful of beings who can call down Armageddon, and from the looks of things, you just did it. Congrats. Now, until we have more information, you should probably play mute."

That was good advice.

For once, he'd take it.

At first, Nick just thought the storm he'd seen earlier had arrived. But there was something ominous about this one. A heaviness to the air that wasn't quite right. Every part of him sensed it. And he wasn't alone. Everyone in the school seemed to be on edge, all of a sudden.

As the storm picked up volume, and the hail started striking the old brick building with enough force to shatter windows, teachers brought students out to the hallway in a tornado-style drill.

Nick slid his gaze to Kody. "You know, I've been through more than my fair share of hurricanes and tornadoes. . . . I ain't never heard anything like this. What about you?"

"Sounds Apocalyptic."

And since she'd been through one or two of them, she'd know.

She gave him a hard stare. "When you and Caleb closed the hell-gate and released your father's powers, you are sure you sealed it properly? Right?" she asked again.

He gave her a droll stare. "Are you seriously asking me if I said all the words? 'Cause yeah, I basically said it. Yeah. Almost in the right order. With all the right syllables."

She rolled her eyes at his play on one of his favorite movies, *Army of Darkness,* that he'd made her see enough times that she now groaned out loud at the mere suggestion of it. "Yeah, it was definitely an N word . . . necktie . . . nickel . . . nectar."

"Nekoda."

"Not funny . . . Nick."

"Yeah, I know. I suck as a dung-eating boyfriend."

Kody snorted. "No. There, you don't. Other departments . . ." She rocked her hand at him.

"Thanks."

She flashed an attractive grin and winked. "Any time, baby. Any time. Hail to the queen."

Suddenly, Stone started making a low howling noise from where he stood with his class, lined up against the opposite wall. And he wasn't the only one. Mason. Alex. Justin.

Every one of the shape-shifters. They were all but whining and barking.

Well, that can't be good. Especially when added to everything else that had already happened. It was as if they were reacting to something only their animal senses could detect. Like the way animals fled or panicked before natural disasters.

This just keeps getting better and better.

The teachers and staff who doubled as Squires, and knew about the preternatural students, began to get nervous that the shape-shifters were about to expose themselves to the "baretos" or normal humans who knew nothing about the supernatural world that co-existed with them and attended St. Richard's. The Squires were all charged with protecting and concealing the identity and existence of the Were-Hunters.

"Attention, students!" Mr. Head said over a bull-horn as he walked down the hallway. "Your teachers will be dividing you into groups for either the cafeteria or the gym until such a time as we have power restored. Please move quickly and quietly to your assigned area."

Nice. Good way to divide out the student body without the baretos being the wiser. This way if something caused the preters to break into their animal bodies, it wouldn't freak out or endanger the uninitiated. Or betray the existence of the Were-Hunters.

Unfortunately, because the staff members didn't know better and had no idea she was actually a corporeal ghost, Kody was placed in the baretos group. Nick, who worked part time as a Squire for an immortal warrior, was sent to the gym with the shape-shifters and the humans who knew about them. It was so aggravating to keep secrets. But as much as the humans thought they knew, there was a lot more to this world than even *they* suspected.

And no one could ever know who or what Nick really was. Not with the bounty on his head. Even a Squire might be tempted to take a shot at him. There were very few he could trust with that knowledge.

As Nick entered the gym, Brynna, whose entire family had been Squires for generations, sidled over to him. "Scary, isn't it?"

"Highly unsettling." Nick glanced over to Stone, who seemed to be struggling to hold on to his human form. He was sweating and shaking. Pale. While the two of them had never gotten along, Nick almost felt sorry for the werewolf.

Nah, not really. Stone was too much of a pack animal bully for that. He enjoyed using his superhuman strength and psychic powers to push others around.

As if on cue, Stone shoved his girlfriend, Casey, back when she moved to check on him, and growled ferociously at her.

Casey screwed her face up as she twisted her arm out of his fierce grip. "Ugh! Hope you die from whatever rabies ails you, Stone."

Stone hissed at her, then grimaced at Nick. "What you looking at, trailer park?"

Not much.

But that made Nick curious about one thing.

"Hey, Bryn . . . if the Were-Hunters break into their alternate forms, how much human would be left in them?"

She glanced over to Stone. "In theory, especially in the case of Stone, those who have human hearts would remain cognizant of their behavior and in control of themselves." Her gaze went to Alex Peltier. "Those who are Katagaria . . ." They were the ones who held animal hearts and weren't as human as their Arcadian cousins.

"Let me guess. We'd be on their menu?"

"Like Brian on Scott," she said, using the name of the football player who'd taken a bite out of his best friend after he'd played Madaug's demon-enchanted Zombie Hunter game. "But we do have enough Squires here that they should be able to quell them before that happens."

"The *should* in that sentence doesn't inspire a lot of confidence in me."

She laughed before she turned toward LaShonda to discuss homework.

The demon sense inside Nick picked up on something. He wasn't sure what. But he'd learned from past encounters to pay heed to that prickly sensation. It was worse than Spidey sense.

Especially with the weather outside so unnatural while he felt it. It was just such a state as this that had heralded the arrival of Zavid when the Aamon had been sent after him. And not to play Parcheesi and watch videos.

Again, he felt that weird slowdown of time before everything sped up like some kind of computer game lag.

What the heck?

His vision darkened in that peculiar way that let him know he no longer saw the world around him as a human being. He was now viewing the world with his perspicacity.

That wasn't unusual.

Nah. What freaked him was the sight of the odd creatures moving through his classmates and around them as if searching for something very specific. Huge and birdlike, they reminded him of mummified plague doctors that were armed with adamantine sickles and wearing black cavalier hats and saturated in blood.

Invisible to the rest of his class and teachers, they paused and turned in his direction. Then, in the next heartbeat, they headed straight for *him*.

CHAPTER 3

Ready to battle, Nick stood up on the bleachers as two of Satan's plague doctors came up to sniff at him while four more hung back, unseen and undetected, to float around his classmates like freaked-out Kabuki dancers. The one thing he'd learned over the last couple of years while dealing with preters was to be ready for anything.

But don't start nothing with them until you had to.

Though to be honest, it was really hard to not shove them out of his personal space. Especially when they practically buried their wrapped, bloody beaks in his armpits.

Not to mention the other no-zone of his body they were headed for.

"Nick, don't move."

He saw Kody's ethereal form on his right. *What are these things?* he projected his thoughts to her.

"Zeitjägers."

I just love it, cher, *when you say things like I ought to know what they are.*

One of them rudely poked his shoulder.

He barely caught himself before he taught the hideous thing some manners.

"Just relax, Nick. I don't think they're here for you."

Don't think or don't know?

Before Kody could answer, Ms. Pantall stood up to glare at him from the lowest bench. "Nick? Do you have a problem?"

He slid his gaze to the huge sickle that was still coated with the blood of the last victim the demons on each side of him had beheaded. That blood was also smeared all over the bandages and clothes wrapped around the two of them and dripping onto the bleachers.

Yeah, he had two very *big, ugly* problems.

Unfortunately, his teacher couldn't see either of those problems or the sickles they carried. Probably a good thing she didn't see the blood, for that matter. Nick tried to stay as still as possible. Maybe they were like bulls and only attacked things that moved. "No, ma'am. Just having some growing pains. Trying to stretch them out a bit."

"Sit your butt down, Gautier, or you'll be running drills during practice till you drop!"

Nick cringed at Coach Heffron's sharp bellow. "Yes, sir."

One of the demons pointed at Nick's foul orange shirt and made a noise that sounded suspiciously like laughter before it stepped back and they moved away from him. Great. Even the seriously jacked-up horror movie rejects mocked his wardrobe.

Thanks, Mom. My future therapist will appreciate the business.

Torn between being relieved and offended, Nick sat down.

Kody's astral projection moved to sit next to him. "You okay?"

He gave a subtle nod. *Just a little offended. So . . . what's a* zeitjäger? *And do they have anything to do with Caleb's sudden onset of projectile vomiting?*

"I doubt they have anything to do with Caleb's sickness. My fear is that they might be here for you and they don't know it yet."

Meaning?

"They're time sentinels, Nick. They guard it, monitor it, protect it, and punish those who abuse it."

Another bad feeling went through him as she said that. "Is that why I haven't heard anything from Ambrose?" Ambrose was his future self who had tricked and killed a demon to steal enough power that he could come back in time and try to save the life of his mother and change his destiny so that he didn't destroy the world.

So far, Ambrose had only mucked things up worse.

Together, they were supposed to be trying to unravel this gnarled mess that was Nick's life and future.

But it'd been some time since Ambrose had made an appearance. The last time Nick had seen him, Ambrose had confessed that he was on the brink of slipping and turning into the demonic Malachai that would destroy the world and end everything and everyone.

Even himself.

Every day that passed without any word from Ambrose made him wonder what his future self was up to.

If Ambrose had given in to their horrific destiny.

Nick stared at the overhead windows where lightning flashed and thunder clapped like cannon fire. Today, it wasn't looking good for either of them.

And he really didn't relish the thought that he would one day usher in Armageddon and unleash an army of ancient ticked-off demons onto the innocent world. An army that would claim the life of everyone Nekoda loved . . .

As well as Nekoda herself.

It was a terrifying and sobering thought that he could become that monster. That was not what he saw when he looked in a mirror and it was not what he wanted to put on his résumé for his future plans.

Suddenly, Mason let out a howl and turned from human to wolf. The students closest to Mason screamed out loud and bolted fast from the bleachers to the floor.

Stone and Alex penned the wolf between them, while the teachers tried to decide how best to handle this. Personally, Nick would have voted for running and screaming like a cheerleader in a cheap horror movie. But apparently, they were a little more sophisticated than that.

"Squires!" Ms. Pantall clapped her hands together to get their attention. "I need all of you to head on home. Don't worry about school until tomorrow. Brynna? Can you go to the cafeteria and let Mr. Head and Sister Katherine know to dismiss those students and call for buses? Tell him what's going on, and we'll hold the Weres here until their parents can come get them. We won't be putting any of them on buses, given the risk factor. They should be fine in here with us until their parents arrive." Biting her lip, she looked at Mason, who was snarling and trying to bite at Stone, and said, "I hope," under her breath.

Nick wasted no time heading for the cafeteria to

pick up Kody's corporeal form. She was already back in her body, waiting for him, right inside the doors as the rest of their class rushed past him in their eagerness to vacate the building before the principal changed his mind and made them stay.

Or worse, someone assigned them homework.

He cringed as the storm outside picked up its fury. "Not sure it's a good idea for anyone to be out in this."

"Yeah," Kody agreed. "But not sure how wise it is to be in here with Mason already shifted, and the others on the verge of turning into animals, either."

No sooner had she finished her sentence than a pack of wolves came tearing down the hallway.

Since they were in the cafeteria, out of the line of sight, the wolves ran past them, toward the exposed students who were at their lockers.

Ah, crap.

The wolves attacked without pause. The humans screamed and ran for cover as best they could. Some even tried to climb straight up the lockers.

Wincing, Nick knew he couldn't stand by and do nothing. Before he could move, Kody grabbed an unattended lacrosse stick and ran after them to protect the humans.

By the time Nick caught up to her, she was barely holding the wolves off. Stone—he could tell by the size, color, and ferocity of the beast who'd attacked him on previous occasions—had the scoop in his massive jowls and was trying to wrench it free to bite Kody. It was so tempting to send a jolt through him and watch him change into a naked human in the middle of the hallway. Only the screaming, fleeing baretos kept Nick from it. While Nick might want to traumatize Stone to get back at him for all the times he'd embarrassed Nick in public, no need in sending the innocent into therapy.

Or blinding himself with the unwanted sight of Stone's hideous naked body.

Instead, he whistled for the wolves and then ran so that they'd chase him back toward the gym. They wasted no time in coming for him like he was the only bowl of Alpo to be had. It was a pants-wetting kind of intensity.

And as Nick slid through the gym door and Mason

sank fangs into his arm, he regretted that decision in the worst sort of way, especially since the room was filled with witnesses who prevented him from using his demonic powers to get Mason off him.

Dang you, nonsensical rules of sanity! Dang you all!

Mason dragged him down hard. Nick tried to pry his arm free as the rest of the pack descended on him with vicious bites.

Yeah, this had definitely been a better idea in the abstract. The reality was much more painful than he'd imagined and it made him really miss Caleb. At least with Caleb around, his enemies had another moving target to chase and chew on.

"Get off him!" Kody tossed a net over Mason she must have manifested out of the sight of the others. She dragged him away from Nick.

Stone went for her throat. Reacting on pure instinct and forgetting the rules about using magic in plain sight, Nick threw his hand out and zapped him. The bolt sent Stone skidding into the bleachers, where he flashed from human to wolf and back again.

Nick started to panic about his slip until Kody distracted them with a scream. As the teachers and adult Weres took over herding the wolves, he saw that the *zeitjägers* were back and watching everything closely.

Too closely for Nick's sanity.

Without a word, Kody pulled him into the hallway, out of the line of fire.

Nick took a second to make sure no one could overhear them. "What are the odds that one of the Were-Hunters made a bad time jump and that's what brought out our ugly giant plague doctors?"

"Sadly, the young Weres do that all the time. No. Something much more treacherous is going on here."

"Like . . ."

"No idea. But it has to be bad. I've only heard of *zeitjägers* appearing in number right before something catastrophic."

And given the fact she was a warrior who'd been killed during Armageddon and sent back in time to stop it from happening, that basically said it all.

They were screwed.

Sighing, Nick looked up at the ceiling. "I swear, if I survive this, I will never, *ever* say that a day is going good again in my life. Lesson learned. *All* days suck from now on."

As the adult Squires began to arrive to evacuate the school, Nick saw Bubba Burdette come in among them. At six foot four and being a former college football linebacker turned zombie-survivalist, Bubba tended to stand out even in a crowd. He was a strange combination of horror-movie buff and redneck, complete with a well-trimmed beard and black hair.

But the one thing *everyone* knew about Big Bubba Burdette, he hated mornings with a burning passion. The fact that he was awake and here at this ungodly early hour more than anything else confirmed that the end of the world was upon them.

His heart pounding, Nick met Kody's gaping expression. "What new hell-monkey wakens?"

Bubba snorted at his sarcasm. "After all the weirdness of the last few days and what with this storm moving in like it did and throwing down hailstones the size of baseballs, me and Mark wanted to make sure you and your mom were safe. I left him with Cherise and promised her I'd see you home." He scowled as he saw the blood on Nick's arm from where Mason had taken a bite out of him. "What happened? Do we need to get you to a hospital?"

That mixture of raw fear and concern in Bubba's blue eyes caught Nick off guard. When Nick had been sucked into an alternate universe, Bubba had been his real, natural father there. A part of him he didn't want to acknowledge had kind of liked it. Since his own dad had spent the majority of Nick's life incarcerated or trying to kill him, Bubba had been the only real father figure Nick had ever known.

At least until two years ago when the immortal Dark-Hunter Kyrian had saved his life and given him a part-time job. Now Kyrian was like a second dad to him, which, while annoying at times, was also kind of nice.

There was nothing Nick wouldn't do for either man.

"I'm fine. Just a flesh wound."

Bubba narrowed his gaze on him, then looked at Kody. "Is he lying to me, Ms. Kody?"

She flashed a playful grin. "Doubtful. You know

Nick. If it was really bad, he'd be whining like a baby and begging for his mom, and a lollipop and sticker."

Bubba laughed before he took Nick's backpack. "C'mon, runt. Let me get you home to your mama. She's worried sick." He glanced around. "So where's your other cohort? Not like Caleb to leave you alone. Way he hangs all over you, boy, I keep waiting for a wedding announcement."

Nick snorted. "Sent home for hurling."

"Lovely."

"Not really. Except for when he scored on the shoes of my least favorite teacher. That was pretty epic."

Bubba shook his head. "Did you drive?"

"Nah. After I got jumped, Ma wants me to, but seriously?" Nick had to force himself to not roll his eyes since he only lived a block and a half away. "Takes longer to find a parking spot than it does to walk it."

This time, Bubba broke out into laughter. "Being the only son of an overly protective Southern mother, I get it . . . in a way only you know. They are truly God's very special creatures."

"Heavy emphasis on the creature part. Especially

those long, clinging, fun-sucking tentacles that wrap around and hold you down till you can't breathe."

"Amen, little brother. Amen."

Kody grinned at them. "Your mama still in town?" she asked Bubba.

"Nah. She left last night. Thank God. I wouldn't want her trying to travel in this mess. I'd be the basket case if she was at the airport today."

"You two," Kody said with a laugh. "I don't know why you pick on your mothers when you're both worse about their safety than they are with yours. Nick, your mom's younger than Bubba and I've seen you hold on to her arm when she's going up and down stairs."

"Hey now, you don't know. . . . I've seen her trip on straight ground. Many times. She could fall. Hurt her arm. Then I'd have to actually wash a dish for myself. God forbid *that* humanity! I'm not even sure how to work a sink. Could fall in and drown myself on accident or something."

Laughing even harder at something she knew wasn't true since Nick washed dishes most nights while his mom worked, Kody shook her head. "Like I said.

Neither of you has room to complain about them being overprotective."

Nick paused as he reached the doors and saw the storm outside. The sky was pitch black. The rain and hail hit the building so hard, it sounded like gunfire. He scowled at the sight of the rain's red spatter patterns. "Is that . . ."

"Blood," Kody finished for him. "It's raining blood."

Nick met Bubba's horrified gaze. "Zombies?"

Grimacing, Bubba shoved at him. "Don't sass me, boy. You're not that cute in high heels."

A chill went down Nick's spine as he turned to see the *zeitjäger* behind him, watching them with great curiosity. They had stopped the Apocalypse. He and Caleb had sealed the portal before the ušumgallu could gather and summon their armies to attack.

Why was this still happening?

It made no logical sense. What else could possibly cause something like this to happen?

He looked at Kody. *Are you sure this isn't from the Arelim civil war?*

No, Nick. I have a bad feeling it's from something a whole lot worse.

His stomach shrank with dread as stark cold terror filled him. "What could be worse?" Nick asked without thinking.

No sooner had those words come out of his mouth than a swarm of bat-sized mosquitos swarmed, driving parents, students, Squires, and faculty back into the building. They screamed and ran, fleeing the pests and seeking shelter.

Nekoda glared furiously at him. "What did I tell you about saying things like that, Nick?"

Not to be stupid. But that was like asking him not to breathe. It seemed to come a little too naturally to him most days. "At least they're not loc—"

She covered his lips before he could say finish saying "locusts." Which was probably a good thing given what kept happening to them. But . . .

Nick stumbled back as a weird feeling came over him. One second everything was weird.

The next, it went dark. He struggled to breathe

against a frigid cold calm that invaded him. It paralyzed every part of his being until he couldn't see or hear.

His eyes rolled back in his head and his knees buckled.

"Nick!" Kody panicked at the way he hit the ground. It was as unnatural as the sudden pallor of his skin. Terrified and shaking, she met Bubba's gaping stare as he knelt beside them.

Bubba gasped in his own alarm. "Nick? C'mon. Talk to me! Say something stupid, boy!"

Yet it was too late. Tears filled Kody's eyes as grief choked her. She couldn't find Nick's pulse in his wrist or neck. He wasn't moving.

Not breathing. No. It couldn't be.

Yet it was.

Nick was dead.

CHAPTER 4

Nick choked and wheezed as someone gave him mouth-to-mouth. "That better be you, Kody. I swear to God if it's Bubba, I'm about to need a truckload of Listerine."

Bubba snorted as he rolled Nick over toward her. "For the record, it was. Again, you ain't that cute in high heels, boy. Though I guess I'd have done it for you if I had to. But only 'cause your mama is, and she'd have stabbed me someplace real uncomfortable with hers if I let something happen to your rotten little hide."

Laughing, Kody brushed the hair back from Nick's face. "You okay?"

"Yeah. What happened?"

Her brow lined with worry, she kept her hand on his cheek. "You stopped breathing and turned a shade of blue I only want to see in your eyes. Not on your skin or lips."

Grateful he'd remembered to shave extra close that morning, Nick rolled to his back and scowled up at his friends, especially as he realized there was a crowd gathered around them. Great. An audience for this embarrassing display. Just what he craved . . .

'Cause puberty just wasn't humiliating enough on its own.

Kill me now.

Bubba held him down as he started to rise. "I've already called an ambulance. You ain't going nowhere till you get checked out. Not with that heart condition you have. My mama *and* yours would slaughter me."

"He's right," Mr. Head said as he pushed through the nosy onlookers. "Don't move, Nick. Just lie still till they get here. Last thing we need's a lawsuit."

Double awesome. More hospital bills. At this rate, he was going to be indentured to the insurance company for the rest of his natural life.

Grinding his teeth, he met Kody's worried gaze. He didn't really have a heart condition, and they both knew it. His early childhood health problems had stemmed from his human body rejecting the demonic parts of his DNA. He was a freak of nature who should have never survived his father's biological gifts.

"Guys, I really do feel fine." He met Bubba's gaze. "C'mon, Triple Threat. Let my Nicky go."

"I'm not chancing it. Nor am I facing your mama without a thorough screening from a licensed doc. I happen to value and appreciate all my body parts being in their current locations."

Nick groaned in agony as he regretted ever allowing Bubba to take his mom out on a date. They'd only gone out once, but since then, Bubba had assumed the role of Nick guardianship with a terrifying iron grip. "Then please don't call her. Go get her and take her to the hospital to meet me. She'll be too tore up to drive and I don't want her out in this mess alone. She drives bad enough as it is."

"Mark's with her. I'll have him drive her over while I follow the ambulance."

Nick gaped at the mere suggestion. "Are you nuts? Have you seen the way that man drives? He's worse than she is. I don't know what loon approved his license, but dang! I swear he found it in the bottom of a cereal box. And he took lessons from Mario and Luigi."

Snorting, Bubba pulled out his cell phone to call Mark and tell him what had happened.

Before Nick could continue his protests, the EMTs arrived. Kody stepped back so that they could check his vitals. With the exception of a fever, they confirmed that there was nothing wrong with him. But because of his heart condition, they insisted that he go in for more testing.

It was so frustrating.

And scary since there was always a chance that they might actually uncover something "abnormal" about him. Something that could land him locked in a lab somewhere for testing since he was about as abnormal as any X-Men could be.

Of course, it didn't help any that he had a new hell-monkey best friend in that one of the *zeitjägers* decided to hitch a ride with them as they took Nick to the ambulance and closed the doors.

Why did *that* have to be his new psycho stalker? Couldn't there by a supermodel somewhere, obsessed with gawky teenage boys with bad wardrobes and velcro-mother issues?

What did it want with him, anyway? And why couldn't anyone else see it?

He stared at the hell-monkey.

The hell-monkey *zeitjäger* twisted the sickle in his hand and stared back.

Very disturbing.

While the EMT kept an eye on his vitals, Nick continued to watch his silent harbinger. Kody slid carefully past it and sat in the corner, out of the way.

Nick glanced pointedly at the *zeitjäger*, then her. *Why is he still with us?*

Kody shrugged. *I can't exactly ask while we have company. If I do that, they might take us both to the psych ward.*

At this point, he was almost willing to chance it. Anything to get to the bottom of what was going on.

"Some weather, huh?" the EMT asked them as they were shut in and the driver took off.

"Yeah." Nick watched as the woman rechecked his blood pressure. "Still a normal teen, right? I haven't mutated into an Avenger or anything?"

She laughed. "Not yet, Tony Stark. Are you trying?"

"Some days. I'd like to try being a billionaire play-boy for a change."

She shook her head. "Well, you might get your chance. Given the size of the mosquitos we had to battle to get inside your school, it wouldn't surprise me if they weren't refugees from a nearby radiated science facility of some kind."

"Probably got into some of my mama's uncle's bayou moonshine. She always said that stuff could bring the dead back to life. And strip the finish off anything, including cars *and* kidneys. Wouldn't surprise me if it couldn't mutate a few skeeters, too."

The EMT laughed so hard, she choked. "Is he al-ways like this?" she asked Kody.

"Yes, he is."

"Girl, you've got your hands full, don't you?"

"You have *no* idea."

And still the *zeitjäger* stared at them as if waiting for something more unholy to happen.

It was so creepy and disturbing. But not nearly as much as the storm that continued to slam against the ambulance until it was forced to slow down to a crawl to get through the streets that were beginning to flood. Even the EMT started sweating.

Their nervousness wasn't helped as the mosquitos began to gather on the outside of the truck to the point that the evil beasts completely covered the windows.

The EMT gulped audibly. "It's like one of them horror movies, ain't it?"

"Yeah," Nick breathed. "And I didn't even play with a Ouija board . . . this time."

Kody snorted. "Maybe this is one of those hundred-year storms or something that drove the bugs out of their nests. You know, the kind of thing that we'll tell our grandkids about?"

The EMT's face paled as more mosquitos hit the

truck. "Maybe, but I've never heard of anything like this." No sooner had she finished those words than something struck the ambulance and sent it careening.

Nick grabbed Kody and shielded her and the EMT as the ambulance turned onto its side and slid down the street. Loose objects flew around them, striking his body and bouncing off them. While the EMT screamed and Kody wrapped herself around him, he used his powers and kept the women safely cocooned and padded from harm until the truck stopped and everything settled down.

For a full minute, he didn't move. Not until the door was wrested off by an unnatural force that skittered down his spine. The EMT shouted out prayers as Kody pushed herself back to deal with their latest threat.

The winds howled. A black smoke rushed forward into the ambulance like giant talons, freezing everything it touched. The EMT shrieked and crawled away from it. She tried to hide as best she could.

Frost covered the ambulance and turned all surfaces white and brittle. Yet they were hot to the touch. Rising up like some ghastly black misty angel, the smoke spread out to form a body and wings. It wore a cowl that covered its head and hid its features.

"Fringe Guard?" Nick asked Kody, assuming it was one of the fierce creatures that protected the boundary between the human world and the spiritual one.

She shook her head. "He's demonic. And he's definitely after you. Probably for the bounty. But not a Guard."

The *zeitjäger* made a hissing noise as it shirked away from Nick's pursuer.

Ah yeah, that ain't good . . .

Nick used his powers to daze the EMT so that she wouldn't understand what was happening or see anything clearly. The last thing any of them needed was for a professional baretos to see what was going on and lose her mind over it. Most people couldn't handle what they dealt with on a day-to-day basis.

He pulled back slowly from Kody. "Why's the *zeitjäger* afraid of my new friend?"

"I don't think he is."

She might be right. The *zeitjäger* seemed to be waiting for Nick to die.

Sorry to disappoint. He wasn't about to go down today, especially not for this ugly beastie. And not for something as ridiculous as money.

Rising to his feet, he blasted the demon back and slammed his fist into its jaw. Yeah okay, that seriously hurt. He'd cry about it later. . . .

If he survived.

With a fierce shriek, the thing manifested a sword. It turned and narrowly missed taking Nick's head.

Nick ducked, but Kody caught the blade with her own sword before it could kill him, and kicked the demon back, out of the ambulance and into the streaming rain. The two of them went at it. He started to help and stopped himself, knowing she could handle it and wouldn't appreciate his interference any more than he would. Besides, she was much better with a sword than he was, since she had centuries more experience using one, and they'd made a pact to never tread on each other's expertise in a fight. He respected her abilities and she respected his.

Instead, he went to check on the EMTs to make

sure they were okay and stable, and that more help was on the way for them.

As he moved past the *zeitjäger*, it cocked its head to stare at him.

"What?" Nick asked it in a challenging tone.

It vanished instantly.

So did the mosquitos, and the rain slacked off, too. Yeah, okay, that was just weirder than holding Mardi Gras in June. Finding snow in August. Or Bubba in a tie and business suit. Made no sense whatsoever.

Trying not to think about it, he moved to help the EMT who'd been tending him. She was shaken up and still dazed, but appeared to be physically okay. He left the rear of the ambulance to check the driver, who was unconscious. Worse, the driver was wedged in the wreckage and trapped behind the wheel. Since Nick couldn't get him out, Nick returned to the rear to look for some way to cut the driver's seatbelt, and pry the wheel away from his body.

While Nick searched, Kody quickly dispatched the demon. As soon as she finished, she returned to his side, but they had no way of freeing the trapped driver, so they took turns maintaining pressure on a tourniquet against the driver's wound where he'd been injured in the crash. The other EMT kept checking on the ETA for another ambulance.

Kody frowned as she scanned the street while they listened to all the calls on the ambulance's radio. "I thought Bubba was following us?"

"We must have lost him in the rain."

Kody used her powers to disguise her sword as an umbrella that she held over him and the two EMTs. "What happened to the *zeitjäger*?"

"Don't know. He vanished."

Crossing her arms over her chest, she shivered. "This is bad, Nick. *Real* bad."

"I know, *cher*. I can feel it."

She jerked her chin toward the smoldering remains of the demon she'd dispatched. "They're coming for you, Nick. Harder and stronger than ever before." She shivered. "Not just Noir. This is . . . I don't know. It's not normal. It's unlike anything I've ever felt before."

Oh goody. Just what he wanted to hear. That made his day all the brighter.

Nick fell silent as he heard the next call on the radio and the address for it. It was one he knew all too well.

His heart stopped beating in stark cold terror as he met Kody's shocked expression. "That's my mom!"

Laguerre smiled at Grim as she entered his office and found him at his desk. "Our friend just returned home with a gift for us. The king is in check."

A slow smile spread across his face. "So soon?"

"Easy enough when you have the pieces all in place. I told you, the Malachai trusts our newest ally. He didn't even see it coming. He has no idea that he's being tested and that if he fails, he loses *everything*."

So it seemed. "Where's his mother?"

An evil laugh escaped her beautiful lips. "Someplace safe."

Grim winced at the thought of the last place anyone would look for Cherise Gautier. "Gah, I hate that hole."

"Most beings do. It's why it was chosen for her prison. He'll never find her there."

Grim saluted her for her cold, calculated choice. "What if our king chooses to sacrifice his queen to the cause?"

"He won't. She's his raison d'être. Nick would give us his Arelim love before he'd allow his mother to die. Whoever controls Cherise, controls Nick. You know that."

"But have you ever wondered why?"

Laguerre scowled. "What do you mean?"

"Think about it. First Adarian gives his life for her, and now Nick. What is so special about this one particular human that two Malachais are willing to kill themselves to keep her safe?"

She shrugged. "Love. It's a useless, pesky emotion to feel. Adarian fell in love with her, and for that pathetic reason, valued her life over his own. Nick, because she's his mother and he adores her. Even more ridiculous, if you ask me."

And still that seemed too simple for Grim to accept it. Why would Adarian care? What would make a creature so foully cruel and uncaring, so selfish and cold, take notice of a tiny, frail woman? While Cherise was attractive, there were millions of other women who were more so. Millions of women who would have appealed to a Malachai.

What had been so special about her that Adarian, after so many centuries of being so careful, would claim her as the mother of his heir?

And then to protect her to such an extent, that he'd ultimately died for her? It just didn't make sense. It never had.

No, there was more to this. There had to be.

More to Cherise Gautier than a simple frail human mother.

Anytime Grim had ever threatened to harm or even approach Cherise, Adarian had gone nuclear. In this game of life and death, of winner-take-the-world, she had been completely off-limits to all of them. The one card no one could play.

The one ace that would make Nick fold.

Now . . .

Grim finally had her in his hands and it was time

he learned why this woman, alone, held the ultimate sway over the two most powerful Malachais who'd ever been born.

She'd already caused the death of one.

And she was about to be the death of the other.

CHAPTER 5

Nick used his powers to shield his presence from the police who had the small parking lot for his condo cordoned off. Dazed and pale, Bubba sat beneath a large black umbrella on the wet back door stoop Nick had sprinted down just a short time ago as he headed off to school. He held a bloodied Georgia Tech baseball cap that Nick knew belonged to Mark while he talked to the police and answered their questions.

Sick to his stomach, Nick listened for details about what had happened.

"I can't believe this." Bubba wadded the black cap in his fist as he looked around the parking lot. "Can I go now?" he asked the cop who was interviewing him. "Mark don't like hospitals, and I don't want him waking up alone in one. More than that, I don't want Nick finding out about his mama from a stranger. That boy don't need no more hurt on him. He just lost his daddy not that long ago. And he thinks the world of his mama. This is the last thing that boy needs to hear when he's off by himself. He's just a kid. I don't want him to think he's alone in the world when he's not. He needs somebody at his side right now, helping him make some sense of this."

The police officer nodded. "We have everything we need. You're free to go."

As Bubba headed for his SUV, Officer Davis stopped him. "Burdette, let us do our job. There's no need for you to get involved in this. We'll find her."

Fury darkened Bubba's eyes. "You better. Otherwise this isn't going to be a mugging and missing persons report. It'll be a homicide investigation, and I can assure you, you won't ever find a body."

"Boy, you better remember you're talking to law enforcement."

A sinister smile curved Bubba's lips. "Yeah. I know. Same law enforcement that never caught the ones who killed my wife and son. And that ain't happening to Nick. He don't deserve that. Not while I'm here to stop it. So you better find whoever did this before I do. 'Cause I promise you, there won't be enough left of them to ID when I get my hands on them. Now, if you don't mind, I'm going to check on my friends and let them know I'm here for them."

Horrified and trembling over what he was seeing and hearing, Nick couldn't breathe as he watched Bubba get into his SUV and drive off.

Someone had taken his mom? For real?

"I'm so sorry, Nick."

Unable to cope with it all, he barely registered Kody's heartfelt words. His mind was whirling too fast. Unlike the police and Bubba, he knew they weren't looking for human perps. A human would never have gotten past Mark. His friend was too well trained and skilled for that.

No. This had the stink of supernatural all over it.

Was that why Caleb was sick? Why the weather

was so bad? Why that crazy demon had come after him in the ambulance and the killer mosquitos had attacked?

Had it all been a distraction? Something to keep them away from Nick's home so that his enemies could draw her out of their protected condo and kidnap his mom?

Would they dare, knowing that once Nick had her free of their grasp, he'd tear them to pieces?

Messing with the Malachai was a dark, dangerous thing for anyone to do. Especially when Nick didn't have full control over that part of himself. More like the Malachai controlled him right now, which made him akin to Cujo on steroids, with a Godzilla complex.

Whenever it broke free, there was always a chance that he might not recover and that it would take him over completely. That he'd never be him or human again. While Noir might think he could control him, Nick wouldn't play that bet. If the ancient god couldn't control his father back in the days when the god had more strength, odds were he'd never be able to leash the Ambrose beast now that Noir had spent countless centuries growing weaker.

But none of that mattered right now. Only his mom did.

Nick winced as panicked fear for her consumed him. How could this have happened? They purposefully kept his home shielded. No one should have been able to find his mother. No one knew he was the Malachai. Or even where he lived.

That's not true.

One very evil little beastie was currently residing in his home. Xev knew exactly who and what he was.

How important his mother was to him.

Bile rose in his throat as he remembered the warnings Caleb had given him about saving Xev and taking him in. He was the only "enemy" who knew all about Nick and where he lived and breathed. How to "cripple" him. Xev had betrayed the good guy side to Noir once before. He'd supposedly led their enemies straight to his own family to be slaughtered by Noir's army. It was why Caleb had refused to allow Xev to live in his home, even though they were brothers.

Why Nick had been forced to keep the Šarru-Dara—the Malachai's blood general—in his condo. Caleb wouldn't allow Xev anywhere near him without viciously attacking him.

If Xev could do that to Caleb . . .

Xev's betrayed me. Just like Caleb had said he would.

No good deed goes unpunished. It was something both his boss, Kyrian, and Acheron had said to him, repeatedly.

Kody bit her lip. "Nick? What are you thinking? What's that look mean?"

Furious, he ignored Kody as he teleported into his room. With his vision darkened by Malachai bloodlust, Nick found Xev right where he'd left him when he headed off to school. Asleep in his bed as if everything was right in the world. Like nothing bad had happened.

That only added to his rage. How dare the ancient being lie here as if the world wasn't in chaos! As if his mother hadn't been taken by God only knew who or what. She be could dead already.

Tortured . . .

Wanting blood and vengeance in the worst way, Nick growled low and yanked the blanket off him.

Xev came awake with an equal amount of defiant fury. Turning and flipping into a crouch, he hissed like a cat, exposing a set of jagged teeth. His rusty-sea-blue eyes held a diamond-shaped pupil as he angled his arm up to blast Nick, only to realize who his attacker was. Since he was enslaved to the Malachai, he couldn't physically hurt him. So his eyes and teeth returned to normal while he braced himself for Nick to beat him. It was what Nick's father would have done to him for the affront.

But as Nick saw the deep, vicious scars that marred every inch of Xev's lengthy body, and in particular the two that marked where his wings had been savagely ripped off his back as punishment for his crimes, he calmed down.

While Nick had no doubt that Xev was a fierce, deadly creature capable of ruthless violence and betrayal, he no longer thought he was responsible for his mother's abduction. Surely Xev wouldn't have gone back to sleep after taking her. That would have been all kinds of stupid.

And Xev was anything but dumb.

Had he taken his mom, he'd have known to run to the highest hills he could find for fear of what Nick would do to him once he found out about it.

Kody drew up short as she entered the room behind Nick and saw Xev huddled naked on the bed. Squeaking, she quickly turned around and dodged back into the hallway. "Sorry, Xev."

Still Xev didn't move or speak as he stared up at Nick with a brutal intensity that waited for Nick to unleash his worst wrath on him.

And that, too, drove the last of the Malachai anger out of Nick. Having been misjudged by most everyone around him, he wasn't real big on doing that to others. He handed the blanket back to Xev. "Didn't you hear the thunderstorm?"

Xev covered himself. "What storm?" He scratched at his ear, then raked his hand through the garishly bright red and yellow hair he'd been cursed to bear, trying to smooth it down.

"There was hail, pounding thunder . . . a blood rain," Kody said as she came back into the room. She eyed Nick suspiciously. "Are you okay?"

Not really, but Nick nodded anyway since he was no longer on the verge of ripping Xev's throat out, or shifting into his Malachai form. "My mother was kidnapped from the parking lot outside." He glared at Xev. "Did you not hear it?"

Xev brushed his hand over the ancient words bearing his cursed fate that were branded into the flesh of his torso. "You think I did it?"

"I don't know what to think. Honestly, I'm too pissed off to really focus right now. I just want to beat the crap out of someone. And since you're here and taller, bigger, and meaner, you make a good target, bud."

Kody placed a comforting hand on his shoulder. "That's the Malachai talking."

"I know. But knowing doesn't change the fact I want to kick the snot out of whoever did this. Or failing that . . . whoever happens to be close by." Nick locked gazes with Xev. "I just find it odd that no one knew where my mom was until you moved in. Now . . ."

"I swear, I didn't betray you. Why would I?"

"I don't know, Xev. I don't even know who or what you really are. Every time I ask, you dodge the question like a bullet aimed for your temple."

Xev finally stood to his full six-foot-six height. As he gripped the blanket around him, his angry gaze went to Kody, then back to Nick. "Fine. You want the truth? Before my powers were stripped as punishment and I was damned by the Source gods, I was the god Daraxerxes. Cousin and friend to the firstborn Malachai."

Shocked that he finally had an answer about Xev's past, Nick stood there as the truth slowly sank in.

Xev had known the very first Malachai.

Day-yam.

While he'd known Xev was old—the first of the Malachai's generals—he'd had no idea just how old that was, until now. Never would he have guessed that Xev was related to the Malachai demon bloodline.

That he'd actually known Monakribos. "You were there in the very beginning?"

He gave a curt nod. "Even though we'd been friends, during the first war of the gods I fought against the Malachai and his army. Against my own mother and her sister. *I* was the reason your great ancestor was defeated, cursed, and enslaved. It was for that betrayal against them that I was set up, betrayed, and punished by all those I called ally, including my own brother, who will never again have faith in me. For anything. My mother and aunt strove to teach me a vital lesson about trusting others. And it is one I learned well, indeed. No matter how much of yourself you give. No matter how much you bleed. In the end, they believe whatever lie they want to believe about you. They see only the worst, in spite of the fact that you only gave them your best. And there's nothing you can do or say to change another's mind. Ever."

Xev's eyes clearly telegraphed the depth of his anguish. "The real truth never catches up to the venom enemies spew against you. So I don't expect you to believe me about today, or anything else. No one ever has. My mother personally saw to it that no one would ever put me at their back again. Not for any reason."

"Wait," Kody said with a scowl. "The Sephiroth general, Jared, was the one who ended that war."

"No. He naively betrayed his Sephirii army to the dark powers and put down his own soldiers, but I was the god who ended the war by making sure the Mavromino were cut off from this world. So after Braith abandoned her siblings for the deal they made against her child, it was my blood used to seal those original gates to Azmodea. My blood that continues to hold them back from this world."

Kody gasped. "That's why you're the Malachai's blood general. *You're* the one who locked Azura and Noir in their prison."

Xev gave a slow single nod. "And it's my blood, through the Malachai's hand and magic, that's needed to unlock it and release them back into this realm."

Completely still, Nick was trying to digest that and not lose his mind in the process. The Mavromino, which could be both singular or plural, was the essence of all darkness. The great evil that had spawned the three primal dark gods—Azura, Braith, and Noir.

From a forbidden *affaire de coeur* that had ended tragically, Braith had birthed the first Malachai and seen her child cursed by the gods of light, who'd demanded the Malachai's wife and child be sacrificed to appease them. Heartbroken and with no other choice about the matter, Braith had vanished and left her son to become the property of her evil siblings, Azura and Noir.

To never again see her child, if she wanted him to live.

Since the day they'd been locked away from the world of man, Azura and Noir had been trying to get back to it and restart the war they'd lost. Each generation of Malachai had been a tug-of-war of wills between the two ancient gods and the Malachai, who was both a weapon and tool for them. Without Braith, Azura and Noir lacked the total control they needed for the Malachai to make him do their bidding.

No matter how hard they tried, they could never

bring him under full heel. And so the balance between good and evil had been maintained.

Until now.

Nick was a very different beast. No one knew why, but he was much, much stronger than his predecessors. He, alone, could tip the balance into the dark gods' favor and allow them to finally defeat the Kalosum, and forever extinguish the side of light in the world of man.

Worse, something was going to realign in the future that would bring Braith home. Something that would make Nick snap and side with her against the world. Together, they would bring about Armageddon.

No one knew what would cause that, either.

Not even Ambrose.

But it was coming.

All they knew for a fact was that Noir and Azura were hell-bent on claiming Nick as soon as possible. . . . That if they were to lay hands on him, he'd be in worse shape than Xev, and he'd never again know freedom.

Never again be human.

Yet there was also a prophecy that said Nick was the only Malachai who could change and become a force for good. If they could find a way to anchor him to the Kalosum, they could forever alter the course of history.

It was all up to him, and him alone. But it was something much easier said than done since the Malachai was born of pure wroth and hatred—born of violence to do violence. His nature was to harm and spew venom. To kill and to maim. Kindness and love didn't come easy to him. None before Nick held any understanding of those words. The only reason Nick did was because of his saintly mother.

Should he ever lose her . . .

Everything would come undone. He would lose himself to the darkness and become the soulless Malachai. An unfeeling, invincible killing machine.

Kody laughed nervously as she faced Xev. "Sheez. No wonder Caleb was so nervous about you being free."

Nick frowned. "What do you mean?"

She released a deep breath. "Don't you see, Nick? Xev's one of the keys to unleash Noir and Azura. It's what makes his being free so dangerous. So long as Xev remains in this dimension, you're just one step closer to being the very thing you don't want to become. He's not just a god. He's a key."

Maybe, but throwing Xev into a pit and locking him there to be abused when he'd done nothing to deserve it didn't seem like the way to redemption, either. To him, that lack of regard for someone else's life and well-being was more in line to becoming the Malachai than his stupidity in taking a chance on someone who appeared to need kindness, even though everyone said he shouldn't.

So long as this act of charity only bit Nick on the butt, and not someone he cared for, he could live with the consequences. He didn't want to be *that* guy who let other people make up his mind for him.

But there was one question he had for Xev. "Who's your mother?"

Xev pointed to his vivid blue eyebrows—another

part of his curse—and spoke the last name Nick ever expected to hear. "Azura. Firstborn of all evil, she seduced my father, Verlyn, in an attempt to control and manipulate him. I was nothing but a tool to her and a source of continual aggravation to my father, who despised me for binding him to her." He swallowed. "Like you, I was born of two warring natures that constantly pull at me. But unlike you, I never chose good out of any kind of loyalty or decency to the Kalosum. Rather, I did it defiantly as a way of striking back at my mother, and making her regret and curse my conception and birth."

"And what of your father?" Kody asked.

Xev laughed bitterly. "What of him?"

"Aren't you loyal to him?"

His features turned to stone as he glanced away from them. "After what he and Caleb did to me, I have loyalty to nothing and no one. We have a mutual understanding. Verlyn never wanted to be my father. I never wanted to be his son." But Nick didn't miss the pain that lay beneath the dry delivery of those words.

Their rejection had hurt Xev so deeply that he'd been left with the same choice Nick had faced with his own father.

Deny any want of love. It was easier that way. To pretend you didn't care. That you didn't need or want your father. But deep down in places you didn't want to own up to, you knew the truth. It always cut and bled. An open wound that wanted what they would never give.

A single damn about you.

And that was why Nick couldn't turn his back on Xev. Why he'd kept him here when everyone else told him he was an idiot for it. He knew that same pain too intimately to dole it out to someone else.

He and Xev were brothers in pain.

Brothers in heart.

Nick couldn't throw Xev aside like everyone else had done him and leave him to rot alone. It just wasn't in him to be that cold. His mother had taught him better than that.

Xev locked gazes with Nick. There was so much agony and need inside those hazel eyes that it was hard for Nick to see what he, himself, kept hidden from the world reflected back at him. "I told you when you brought me here, Malachai, that I have no understanding of kindness or love. You should have left me in my prison like all the Malachais before you. It's where I belong. It's all I understand."

Nick heard those words that sent a chill down his spine. They were so similar to what his father had told him from the cradle. *Put no one at your back unless you want them to plant a knife in your spine.*

And yet . . .

He sensed something more inside Xev. His instincts told him that Xev wasn't quite the badass he pretended to be. That there was a vulnerability deep inside him he denied. A need for acceptance that Nick related to. Maybe he was wrong. But every part of himself told him that Xev wasn't quite as evil as the ancient wanted him to believe.

Even if he was the son of Azura.

Of course that was easy for him to say, being the son of the Malachai. He didn't want to be judged for his parentage, either. He wanted to believe they were both better than their genetics.

Besides, Xev wouldn't have fought to save them if he really didn't care. Wouldn't have been wounded protecting them. Nor would he have gone back to save Kody when he could have left her trapped between worlds, forever.

Xev could deny it all he wanted, but he had a heart and he understood decency and kindness both.

Not to mention, he was older than anyone Nick knew, even Acheron, who was over eleven thousand years old. Right now, they needed that advantage. If Xev had known the first Malachai, then maybe, just maybe he would know some way to keep Nick from turning into the monster Ambrose.

It was worth a shot.

And at this point, sadly, it was the only chance they really had.

Nick nudged him toward the closet. "Go on and get dressed, Xev," he said, gently. "We've had a bad morning and my mom's missing. Caleb's sick and—"

"What do you mean sick?" Xev asked, interrupting him.

"He has some kind of cold."

Xev's jaw dropped. "No. It's not possible."

Nick exchanged a frown with Kody as he caught the underlying tone of Xev's voice. "You know what's wrong with him?"

"Are any other gods infected?"

Nick shook his head. "Caleb's a demon, not a god." As soon as he said that, he remembered that wasn't entirely true.

"Malphas is a demigod. We have the same father . . . Verlyn. And while a demon can't get sick, there was an illness my mother crafted that can strike down the ancient gods, including Caleb, should he come into contact with it."

Nick struggled with that concept. "That doesn't even make sense. How could something make a god sick and not a demon?"

"When it's strictly targeted to them. It was biological warfare, designed to take down an entire pantheon at my mother's command. She was rather bitchy that way, back in her time."

Kody gasped in alarm. "Does that include you?"

Xev laughed. "You honestly think my mother

would spare me any pain?" He pointed to the words of his curse on his torso that showed exactly how little his mother had cared whether or not her son was left to wallow in eternal misery.

She winced visibly at his coldly stated answer. "What about Nick? Can it hurt him?"

Xev studied Nick like some science experiment that had been badly mutated. "He might have some immunity now that he's generations removed from the goddess who birthed the first Malachai. That part, I don't know. I'm not even sure it's the same illness as the one I saw on the ancient battlefields. But it's the only thing I can think of that would make Caleb ill. He should be immune from any other known disease."

That at least made sense. Finally. "What of my mother's kidnapping?"

"I know nothing of her being taken. I swear. She was in the kitchen, getting ready for work, when I came in here to sleep. That's all I know of her whereabouts. Had I heard anything, I would have protected her with my life."

Nick inclined his head to him. "All right. Get dressed. We'll be in the kitchen, waiting."

Xev was dressed before he finished speaking. "Show me where they grabbed your mother. I'll see if I can detect anything about her assailants."

Nick arched a brow at Kody. "Dang, I need to remember I can do that when I'm running late to school. Those ninja dressing skills are handy."

She snorted at his misplaced humor.

Nick took them to the rear of the condo, but didn't open the back door since the police were still there. He jerked his chin toward them. "Who or whatever it was attacked her and Mark as they were getting into his Jeep. Busted him up enough that he was sent to the hospital."

A strange look descended over Xev's face.

Nick turned toward Kody. "Is he having a vision or does he need to go potty?"

Kody shoved at him. "Nick," she chided.

"What? It's the same look the toddlers used to get on their faces in the crying room I had to help monitor as part of my charity work when I was going through Confirmation."

She groaned out loud. "You're awful."

"I'm the Malachai, baby." Nick winked at her to let her know his cocky attitude was a joke. "Goes with the territory."

Xev's eyes glowed the same way Caleb's and Nick's did whenever they accessed their powers. *That* was not a joke.

Nor was the dark, shrieking cloud that was headed straight for them.

At first, Nick thought it was another swarm of mosquitos. Yet as it drew closer, the sound was unmistakable.

It was a murder of crows. And not just a standard murder. More like a Quentin Tarantino–style slaughter fest of them. With friends, family, and every feathered acquaintance they'd ever made.

In a mad, gory frenzy, the crows attacked like something out of the old Hitchcock film. They descended on the police and people, who, screaming and cursing, ran for cover while the birds pecked and slashed at them. Thunder and lightning crackled, threatening to dump more rain. Some of the police shot at the birds. But nothing deterred them.

Total pandemonium broke out.

As people flooded into his building for protection, Nick ran through a mental list of his powers. He could talk to the dead and sort of control zombies.

Okay, it didn't work quite the way it should, but it was useless on fowl creatures.

He had partial telekinesis, which was also iffy at best. His grimoire, that was even lippier and more sarcastic than he was. Of course, if sarcasm were lethal, he'd be a legendary killer. Sadly, that skill only served to get him grounded, or added days to his detention. Slammed into lockers by Stone and crew . . .

And it pissed Kyrian and Acheron off to no end.

His sword . . . Not a good idea to pull that out in front of skittish police.

Nothing he had could help with this problem. Not even his wings. He wasn't Dr. Dolittle. He had no control over murderous birds that he knew of. But at least the crows didn't appear to be able to enter the building.

They stopped at the threshold as if the protection spells Menyara and Caleb had put in place were binding for them, too.

Even so, Xev pulled them back, further into the building. "Death," he breathed. "Those are his carrion birds of choice. You think he sent them here?"

Nick went cold at the mention of Grim. "Does this mean he had anything to do with my mother's disappearance?"

Xev considered that. "Or he's looking for you, perhaps."

Kody met Nick's gaze. "Grim does know where you live and who your mother is. What she means to you. Maybe he decided to go rogue, and on the attack?"

Grim also knew that his father was dead. That Nick had come into his full Malachai powers. Though he should be subservient to the Malachai, that really wasn't their relationship.

Death had a massive superiority complex where Nick was concerned.

Even so, it didn't quite add up. Up until now, Grim had been casually insulting and somewhat helpful.

Nick glanced back at the murder of crows that was eyeballing them through the barrier. "But why snatch her and then send those"—he jerked his chin at the crows—"after me? It's not like he doesn't have my phone number. Literally. Had he called, I'm dumb enough to have met him somewhere without the theatrics."

Xev's scowl deepened as the crows moved to sit on the sills of the building as if waiting for something specific to happen. It was so creepy, it made the hair on the back of Nick's neck stand on end.

The ancient god stepped back and paled even more.

Her own features paling, Kody bit her lip at the way Xev reacted to them. "What is it?"

He moved closer to the window, then fell back again. "They're Memitim."

"Mem-a-who?" Nick asked.

"Memitim. They were the soldiers used against

Arelim." He turned to face Nick. "Back in the day, they were under the command of Malphas. They were his army."

"I don't understand."

"Long before Caleb met his wife and decided to live the life of a peaceful farmer, he fought with my mother and *his* against our father. He was one of the Mavromino's greatest and strongest generals. The Memitim were his soldiers that he used against the Kalosum. After centuries of warring against us and laying waste to mankind, he switched sides because of his wife and swore off his sword forever. When the Memitim went after him and refused to let him live in peace, he single-handedly put them down, and they swore vengeance upon him. These are their spirits and they're here to make good on their vow." His gaze burned into Nick. "Someone resurrected them for their revenge."

"How do you know that?"

"You're the Malachai. Listen to them and you can hear it in their cries."

Nick tilted his head as he closed his eyes and did

what Xev said. He opened up the part of himself that honestly terrified him. Anytime he tapped those powers, there was always a part of his heart scared that he wouldn't make it back to be normal again. A part scared that he'd be lost to the darkness forever.

But Xev was right. He could hear them now.

Malphas! We've come for you! It's time for you to pay for what you've done! Come out and face us, you craven dog!

Nick almost told them he wasn't here, that they had the wrong address, then caught himself. Better they stay misinformed. So long as they were surrounding the wrong building, they wouldn't be trying to break into the right one and kill his friend.

Yet one thing he knew for certain. Those crazy, batty crows weren't going anywhere. Not until they had Caleb's heart in their bloody little beaks.

And they had no intention of allowing anyone else to leave the building, either. Something proven when one of the cops tried, and the birds descended on him like a bunch of winged piranhas.

People screamed as two cops shot at the birds in an attempt to drive them off their colleague.

While they were distracted, Nick opened the door to return to his individual condo unit and let Xev and Kody in before they got caught in the cross fire.

Kody stepped away from the door. "I don't understand. If the Memitim want revenge on Caleb, why are they *here*? Shouldn't they be at Caleb's?"

Xev shrugged. "His most recent scent would have been at your school or on Nick. It must be what they locked on to and followed when they were freed. Since they're carrion spirits, they can't come into this building because it's protected. And they can't find him because Nick teleported him to his home, correct?"

"Yeah."

"Then Caleb should be safe. For now."

"Again with the *should*," Nick mumbled. "Really hate that word."

Ignoring his comment, Kody crossed her arms over her chest. "Could they have made Caleb sick?"

"You're focused on the wrong concern." Xev stepped away from them.

"Meaning?"

Xev looked past her shoulder to the window, where more crows were gathering. "It's not whether or not they carried the illness that should concern you. It's who opened the hell-gate that unleashed them."

CHAPTER 6

Nick grimaced at Xev's dire words. "Dude, if my gut draws any tighter, I'm going to pass a diamond soon. So what hell-gate doth thou mean now, my lord demon? Or is it demon lord?"

Xev ignored his sarcasm. "You should know, since you're part of the ušumgallu that controls them. Or, more to the point, the head of the beast."

"Yes, but see, in the midst of my learning all about econ, biology, locker combinations, and American history, they foolishly ignored and neglected this part of my most vital education, and so I'm seriously lacking. Please, do catch me up before any more loathsome creatures come perching on my sill, and singing me such lovely death serenades."

Xev ignored his sarcasm. "You know the story of Pandora's Box?"

"Yeah?"

"It wasn't a box or a jar the curious human opened that unleashed those ill spirits into this world. It was a living membrane she ruptured that could never again be closed or healed. That's why Death, Bane, and War are always in this realm with humanity. Why no one can defeat them or banish them completely. Not even I."

Sighing wearily, Xev closed the curtains to block the crows from seeing into the condo and spying on them. "Because of one woman's defiance of a divine order, mankind was forever condemned to suffer them and their cruelty, with no way to fully banish them from this human plane. Think of it as the eleventh hour for Man. Forever walking hand in hand with their own destruction and death. With humanity's only tenuous hope for salvation being this terrifying thing we call free will. When the first woman so innocently and blindly gave birth to those three, she unknowingly damned this world to disease, war, and death. To the eternal battle for this middle ground and the fate of all humanity. But . . . thanks to the gods who care about her kind and who took pity on them, the other four Snake šarras or chieftains remain supernally bound and contained. Restrained. Each with their own malevolent group they uniquely control as pawns in this eternal war to the one suzerain who leads them."

Kody inclined her head to Nick. "The Malachai." Together with his six main leaders, or generals, they made up the ušumgallu.

Xev nodded. "And Nick, alone, can open the supernal realms and unleash the demons en masse into this world to take possession of it. The Malachai is also the only being who can summon the three of us from our prisons. Me. Livia and Yrre." The eternal balance. Three of the ušumgallu remained in this world—War, Bane, and Death—while the other three remained in stasis. "No one save the Malachai can ever unlock our gates. But it's not an easy task."

Nick frowned. "I've wondered about that. Why has no Malachai before me ever let you guys out?"

"For many reasons. One, it's too draining for the Malachai. There's always a risk that as soon as he frees us, one of us or another might kill him before he recovers enough strength to protect himself. Remember, he's usually a child when he inherits his powers and he can't really control us. If he combines us, it would be easy for us to join together to kill or enslave him. So, the best thing for a Malachai to do is to always put us down . . . like a rabid dog, as soon as he takes his father's life. Never give one of us a chance to go for your jugular. We will take it."

Nick glanced to Kody as a chill went down his spine. He knew how little regard and love Grim and Laguerre had for him, most days. He could only imagine how awful it would be to fall under their "benevolent" control. "Why are you warning me about your friends?"

Xev rubbed at his brow as if he had a sudden migraine. Or possible brain tumor. "To begin with, they're no friends of mine. While I did share kinship with the original Malachai, we were born centuries apart. With the exception of you, I've only met a Malachai long enough for him to yank me from my hole, drain my powers, and return me to hell to recharge until the next *fun* summoning. As for the other šarras, we were enemies in wars where I took great pleasure in kicking their collective asses, so I barely tolerate *them*." He straightened to glare imperiously at Nick. "I was born the son of Verlyn and Azura, and fostered by Inari. Have you *any* idea of the power I once wielded?"

Yeah, that would have been a lot.

Xev passed a bitterly amused glance to Kody. "To give you an inkling, Gautier, I was the only ancient god born who could kill a Chthonian."

Nick's jaw dropped at that. The Chthonians were virtually extinct now, but at one time, they had been a race of god-killers who had once waged their own war against Xev's breed. "Seriously?"

"Seriously. And all that power did was make me a target to everyone around me . . . for one reason or another. It never once brought me any kind of happiness." His gaze burned into Nick with his sincerity. "I don't want to be you, Malachai. Hunted. Hated. Friendless. Without haven. I don't want to be a part of this world . . . or of anything, for that matter. I'm done with it all."

Xev's gaze hesitated at a picture on the wall of Nick's Confirmation, where he stood beside his mother outside of St. Louis Cathedral. His eyes flashed red. "I will help you get your mother back for the same reason I saved Nekoda. You were kind to me and I don't believe in repaying kindness with cruelty. But honestly? All I want is to be left alone and forgotten. I have no use for this world. And even less for you."

Nick frowned. "You really want me to send you back?"

He rubbed at his arm where the ancient symbols of his curse were branded. "When you've lived without kindness for as long as I have, it becomes its own form of cruelty. It stings in its own unique way."

Nick despised the fact that he knew exactly what Xev meant by that. It was the same suspiciousness he had whenever someone complimented him. He was so used to being insulted that if, by some miracle, he actually got a compliment from someone, he analyzed it over and over to see if it was somehow a veiled insult instead.

How sad was that?

But he couldn't help it. The world had predisposed him to expect meanness from strangers. It shouldn't be that way. But it was. It was why Nick went out of his way to try and make people feel appreciated and important. Especially those others tended to overlook—streetcar drivers, doormen, vendors, janitors, bathroom attendants, maids. Hobos.

Everyone mattered.

Kody swallowed hard. "Can I ask a personal question?"

Xev shrugged. "Sure."

"Given that amount of power you were born with . . . how did they ever capture you?"

Agony swam in the hazel depths of Xev's rust-colored eyes. His features turned to stone as a single tear slid down his cheek. "There's the bitterest irony of all. They unknowingly sent the only warrior after me I would never harm."

"Who?" Nick asked.

"The one life I wouldn't take."

"And that was?"

"A life that mattered more to me than my own."

Nick sighed as he passed an irritated grimace to Kody and gave up on the never-ending hamster wheel loop of madness. It was obvious that even now, Xev had no inclination of sharing that identity with anyone. Whoever it was, he intended to let no one use them to hurt him again.

He could respect that, too.

Given that, Nick changed the subject. "So which of the gates do you control in this smorgasbord of fun-filled nightmarish holocaust?"

"The prison realms of the cursed gods. Both good and bad. I can bring them all back into play and return them to war against each other."

Kody gestured toward the window. "And the Memitim? Who holds their key?"

"The souls of the dead are controlled by Yrre. She's the one who would have unleashed them against Caleb."

Kody went pale. "Nick saw her earlier."

"What?"

Nick nodded. "In the hallway at school. Right before Caleb got sick."

"And neither of you mentioned it before now?" His tone betrayed his outrage.

"I thought I was hallucinating."

Xev arched one arctic blue brow. "You do that a lot?"

"Here lately? More than I want to cop to. Let us not forget that I *just* got back from an alternate universe. While I like to think I'm adjusting pretty well to that, I do still have some lingering issues."

Xev cursed under his breath.

"But the gates were sealed shut after his father died," Kody insisted. "Caleb wouldn't have made that mistake. He knows the severity of those consequences."

Xev ignored her outburst. "Are there any other hallucinations I need to be aware of?"

"Aside from you—the cat that drinks up all my

milk in the middle of the night while I sleep—suicide crows, ghost riders in the school hallway, killer mosquitos, and plague doctors, I think we're covered. Unless you want to count the rampaging teenage werewolves." He glanced over to Kody. "Oh, and the ghost girlfriend, of course."

"Plague doctors?" Xev scowled. "What are plague doctors?"

Nick snorted. "That's all you got out of my rant? Really?"

Kody ignored him. "*Zeitjägers.*"

"Why were they there?"

Shaking his head, Nick shrugged. "No idea. They didn't exactly speak. Just stared at me like my mom at a parent-teacher conference where I royally screwed up. And speaking of, none of this is getting me closer to my mom. I'm thinking we should go see Mark and find out what happened, as soon as possible." He peeked through the curtains. "So how do we get rid of or through psycho Daffy Duck out there?"

Kody turned toward Xev. "Nick is still in charge, right? He can stop all this from getting worse?"

"Yes and no. You have to remember, he's not the only creature who can call out Armageddon. . . . He's only *one* of them." Xev grimaced. "Granted, he's a very scary one, but he's not the only threat the world has. And we don't know who or what started this. It might be someone after him, or another entity entirely. Someone or something we haven't even thought about yet."

Nick was so beginning to hate this day. "Look, I don't want to be a threat to anyone, except who or whatever took my mom and hurt Mark and Caleb. I'm an easygoing Cajun. Live and let live. *Laissez les bon temps rouler.* That's my motto. I just want to live my life in peace." He paused. "After I kill whoever took my mama."

Xev snorted. "Unfortunately, with your parentage, it doesn't work that way. But I agree. We need to speak to your strange homicidal duck urine friend about what happened."

"Can we teleport past the Memitim?" Kody asked Xev.

"We should be able to. The worst thing is they might follow the scent, thinking we're Malphas."

"Then buckle up, buttercup. Let's see how bad I screw this up this time." Nick took Xev's arm so that he could flash the two of them to the hospital, since Xev wasn't familiar with the layout of the building. Sad to say, Nick had been there enough over the last couple of years that he was rather intimate with it.

Even so, teleporting was still a risky move, but given the weather and the crows, he didn't want to chance driving there while being dive-bombed by piranha birds.

As soon as they were clear and had materialized at the hospital, Kody appeared right behind them, inside a small broom closet. "Nice choice."

"Yeah, I was aiming for a bathroom and missed. Oh, well. At least it wasn't the lobby and no one's needing therapy from having seen us appear out of thin air. Remind me, I really need to get one of those flashy things they have in *Men in Black*. That could really come in handy for embarrassing mistakes." Nick glanced down and smiled. "And look! I'm fully clothed this time! Awesome! I can be taught!"

Sobering from his rampant sarcasm, he opened the

door and checked the hallway to make sure it was clear before he stepped out and motioned for them to follow. So far, it wasn't too bad. They might survive to make it to dinner.

Nick hoped for the best, but prepared himself for the worst. Just in case. Pulling out his phone, he called Bubba, who answered immediately.

"Boy, where the devil are you?"

He looked about on the drab walls for their location. "Floor three. Where you at?"

"ER, looking for your sorry hide. I swear. You done worried me to death. Taken at least ten years off my life."

"Aw, don't worry, Bubba. I didn't take them off the good end."

"You ain't funny. Now where are you?"

Nick headed for the elevators. "We're on our way. How's Mark doing?"

Bubba hesitated before he answered. "Why you asking about Mark?"

"I know about him and my mom." Nick led them into the elevator. "We heard it on the radio in the ambulance, on the ride over."

Bubba let out a tired breath. "I didn't want you to find out like that, Nick. I'm sorry, son."

"Thanks. So how's Mark doing?"

"They busted him up pretty good, but as soon as they get the X-rays back, they'll release him. Just want to make sure there's no internal damage. What about you? I asked and they said you weren't even here."

"I'm fine. Just worried about my mom and Mark."

Nick stepped out of the elevator and paused. "We're here. Where are y'all?"

Bubba came out a few seconds later to lead them to Mark's room, where he lay with one arm in a sling. His blond hair was brushed back, and one side of his face was swollen and red. Whatever had attacked him had gotten the best of him and then some.

He rubbed sheepishly at his injured arm. "I'm sorry, Nick. You know I wouldn't have let nothing happen to Cherise if I could have stopped it."

Nick inclined his head to him. "I know. So what happened to you two?"

"No idea whatsoever. I'd just opened the door to let Cherise into the Jeep when I heard something shriek out like a banshee. One second I was on my feet, the next I was dating asphalt. . . . I don't even know what hit me. I saw nothing but thick darkness. Like the ground rose up and jack-slapped me."

Nick groaned silently. This told them nothing. They were right back where they started.

Nowhere.

And still his mom was out there.

Unprotected. Alone.

He couldn't bear the thought of something happening to her. All his life, she'd protected him. Guarded him with everything she had. Now he felt completely responsible for her, especially since he was the primary reason she was in danger. If he wasn't her son, no one would ever target her for harm.

I've got to find her.

And yet, in a strange way, he didn't sense that she was in imminent danger. He couldn't explain it. He had an overwhelming need to find her. But at the same time, there was a part of him that seemed to know she wasn't under immediate threat.

It was such an odd sensation. One that made his

skin literally sizzle and crawl. It moved as if it were alive.

Yeah, this was a weird, funky feeling that defied description.

Suddenly, his phone went off. Nick glanced down at the ID to see who it was. "My boss," he said to Kody and Bubba. "Gotta take it." Stepping out of the room, he answered the call.

"Where are you?" Kyrian's stern tone was undercut by a note of hostile concern.

"Hospital."

That only elevated his boss's worried tone. "You okay? What happened? Why are you there? Were you hurt? Was there an accident?"

It took Nick a second to realize that Kyrian wouldn't have any idea what had happened at school or with his mom. His concern came strictly from the shock of hearing that Nick was in a hospital. Period.

"My mom was kidnapped and Mark was assaulted while she was taken."

"What!" Kyrian's roar was deafening. "When did this happen?"

"Right after school started."

"And you didn't call me?"

"I thought you'd be sleeping."

"Nick—"

"Kyrian." He duplicated Kyrian's agitated tone. "No offense, boss, there's not a lot you can do this time of day." As an immortal Dark-Hunter whose job was to protect mankind from the soulless Daimons who preyed on them at night, his boss had a nasty tendency to burst into flames should daylight touch any part of his body. "Not like you can come out and check on me. It's fine, really. Bubba's right here, by my side."

"Still . . . I can call Acheron and have him—"

"Really, it's okay. Why you calling, anyway? You should be asleep." Since Daimons preyed on humans at night and Kyrian couldn't be in daylight, he usually slept all day and didn't wake up until about an hour after Nick showed up for work after school.

"The weather woke me this morning, and when I checked my phone for voicemail, I saw the notice about the Squire alert at St. Richard's. I wanted to check in with you. Make sure I didn't have to start looking for a new Squire. I hate that crap. Hard enough to deal with *you*. Last thing I want to do is start breaking in a new pain-in-my-keister. Gah, I'd have to change all the locks on the house again."

Nick smiled in spite of the awful day and Kyrian's feigned surly tone. He'd gone from having no one look after him to an extended family that still amazed him whenever he stopped to think about it.

"Bad news. Still alive, boss."

Kyrian scoffed irritably at Nick's light tone. "Don't worry, kid. I'll get the Squires looking for your mother, immediately. And Acheron. As soon as the sun goes down, we'll all be on it."

"Thanks. We have absolutely no leads on where to begin hunting her. Any help would be greatly appreciated."

"We'll find her."

Yeah, but in what condition? That was the nightmare that was currently haunting him while he was awake.

"Thanks. Appreciate it."

As Nick hung up the phone, Kody approached to

rub his back. Closing his eyes, he savored the warmth of her touch. His fear and anger churned inside him and he needed her to ground him right now. He wasn't sure what he'd do if she wasn't here to keep him calm.

"Kyrian's contacting Acheron."

He felt her hand tremble at the mention of her uncle. Acheron had no idea who Kody was, which made sense given that she wouldn't be born until centuries from now. They couldn't let Acheron know, either, especially since his brother, Kody's father, was currently being held by Artemis in a hellish prison. It would totally wreck Acheron's world.

For that matter, Nick couldn't imagine how hard it had to be for Kody to be here in this time with her loved ones who had no idea she was related to them, knowing that if they didn't change things, she'd lose them all over again. That if they made one wrong move, she'd never be born at all.

It was enough to make him lose his mind whenever he stopped to think about it.

How could she stand to be near him, knowing he

was the sole reason they would one day die? That he, alone, would one day single-handedly wreck her entire life and everything in it?

Kody's capacity for love defied explanation. It made no sense to him. He doubted if he could be so forgiving in her place. She had every right to kill him.

But then, that was what made her so incredibly special. What made her hold a part of him that no one else ever would. Like his mother, she was a creature of pure light. One who never failed to warm him no matter how beat down or cold he felt. They could always make him feel better. Make him feel important.

Make him feel loved and cherished.

Heroic.

Cupping her chin in his hand, he leaned down to press his cheek against hers and inhaled the warm, vanilla scent of her skin.

"What am I going to do, Kody?"

"What you always do. Fight with everything you have, no matter what they throw at you. Over. Under. Around, or through. There's always a way. . . . Your enemies will not take mercy on you. The world will not take mercy on you. Therefore, I will not be doing you any favors if I take mercy on you."

He laughed at something her brother used to say to her. It was something her brother had learned from their father. "Love you, Kode."

"Love you, too." Rubbing his arm, she stepped back. "You want me to contact Suriyel and see if they know anything?"

He shook his head. "Let's keep the Arelim out of this for as long as we can. If they don't know anything, I don't think we should notify them. Might stir them up. Make them do something stupid. 'Cause while I like to think I own the majority share of that, it's the part I don't own that others do that keeps me up at night, terrified of what they'll do with their portion of it."

"Good point."

Nick glanced into the room where Bubba and Mark were. Guilt gnawed at him as he saw Mark's condition. They were both innocents who'd been caught in the cross fire of his screwed-up life.

Kody and Xev were right. His enemies would never take mercy on him. It was why he had to be so careful who he allowed into his circle. Ever on guard of those he loved best.

So long as he was around them, they were all in danger. And only a tiny handful of them really knew why. The rest, out of necessity, had to be kept in the dark.

Xev came outside. "So what's our next move?"

Before Nick could answer, his phone rang again. It was Caleb's number. Worried his condition had worsened, he clicked it on to find Livia on the other end. "What is it?"

"I found her, Nick."

"What?"

"Your mom. I just got her home for you, and put her to bed. She's asleep, with no idea what happened to her."

Relief slapped him so hard, he staggered back from it. "What? How?"

"I played a hunch and it turned out to be right."

Nick pulled Kody against him and let out a nervous

laugh. "Liv found my mom. She took her to the condo. They're there now."

"Oh, thank goodness! Is she okay?"

"Yeah." For the first time since he'd left school, he felt good again. "Thanks, Livia. I owe you."

"Think nothing of it. I won't let her out of my sight until you get here. Believe me, nothing's going to happen to her on my watch. You can trust me."

"Again, thanks. I'll be home soon." Nick hung up and stuck his head back into the room to let Bubba and Mark know.

"Thank you, Jesus," Mark breathed. "That's the best news I've heard since the garage told me my Jeep wasn't doomed from that electrical fire I started with my cell phone wire that short-circuited."

While that might sound odd to most, that was a testament of supreme love from Mark, who had an unnatural attachment to his old, beat-up Jeep.

Bubba ruffled Nick's hair. "How you holding up?"

"Much better now that I know she's safe, at home. You?"

"Much better now that I know I'm not going to

prison for first-degree murder for killing whoever took her."

Nick laughed. "I hear you."

Bubba nudged him toward the door. "Y'all go on. I know you want to check on your ma as soon as possible. See her with your own eyes. Tell her I'll be over to bug her as soon as I get Mark home and tuck him in."

"Thanks, Dad," Mark said sarcastically. "Can you mop the drool off my chin, too, while you're at it?"

Bubba ignored him. "You need any money for a cab?" he asked Nick.

"Nah, we got it. Stay in touch."

"You, too."

Heading out, Nick texted Kyrian and Acheron to let them know that everything was okay on the home front.

You sure? Kyrian texted back.

All good. Mom's safe at home. It was a false alarm.

Good to hear it. I'll pass it along to the Squires. Let me know if you need anything else. Rosa's on standby, too.

Thanks, boss. As Nick started to slide his phone into

his pocket, he got a text from Acheron, asking about his mom. He paused in the hallway to answer. *I'm on my way to check on her.*

AR. Keep me posted. PN. There's an ill wind blowing. Keep it at your back, Cajun. Call if you need anything. Pax.

Nick returned his phone to his pocket as another weird feeling went through him. One that raised the hairs on the back of his neck again.

For a second, he thought he saw another *zeitjäger* as the time on the clock showed **11:34**.

Kody frowned. "You okay?"

"Strange feeling in my gut."

"I'm really learning to dislike that phrase."

Yeah, he wasn't a big fan of it, either.

She held her hand out to him and Xev. "Let's go see Cherise."

Nick placed his hand in hers and let her take him home. At first, he didn't see or hear anything. The condo was completely still and quiet.

Only that special fissure in the air that was unique to a paranormal entity let him know that there was

something out of place here. And since the only creatures who could penetrate the barriers were those he
approved, he knew it had to be Livia.

Nick rushed to the bedroom to find his mom lying
on her side in the bed, fast asleep. In jeans and a white
blouse, Livia sat in the corner.

She smiled as soon as she saw him. "Ah, so glad
you're home. As you can see, she's fine."

Nick stopped her as Livia started to leave. "Wait."

She rematerialized with an arched brow. "Yes?"

"Where did you find her? Who took her and why?"

Closing the distance between them, Livia placed
her warm hand against Nick's arm and whispered in
his ear. "I hear things others don't know I do. Even
though I'm risking my life to return her to you, I owe
you more than I can ever repay. It is my honor to
serve you, Malachai. But if I were you, I would be very
careful who I trust her with in the future. Who you
put your faith in. You can never be too careful."

The bad feeling in his gut worsened. "What have
you heard?"

She blinked quickly and glanced about nervously

before she whispered her answer. "I can't say exactly. Just be careful. You have many more enemies than even you know."

"Is that what happened to Caleb?"

Livia glanced past his shoulder to the hallway where Kody and Xev waited. "We should talk later." And with that, she vanished.

Grimacing, Nick went to the bed to make sure his mom really was okay. He sank down to his knees by her side before he reached one trembling hand out to touch her soft cheek. It took all of his strength not to gather her into his arms and hold her there in a steel grip like King Kong with Fay Wray and dare anyone to ever try to take her from him again.

Her eyes fluttered open. "Nicky?"

"Hey, Ma."

She frowned at him. "What are you doing here, baby Boo? Shouldn't you be in class?"

"They let us out of school early. Weather knocked out the power."

She sat up and looked around. "Is our power out, too?"

"Don't know. Didn't test it. Just got home and came looking for you." For the first time, he let out a real breath before he launched himself into her arms and held her close.

Holding him tight, she rubbed his back and rocked him. "Nick? You okay, baby? Something happen at school?"

"Yeah. I'm all right. Just missed you."

"Missed you, too." Laughing, she kissed his cheek. "Not sure why I went back to bed, though. Last thing I remember was fussing about the milk. Then I was going for the paper. Hmm . . . must be getting old. Losing my mind."

Nick snorted. "You're not old. That's just me aging you before your time." He winked at her. "By the way, I have friends from school with me."

"Usual suspects? Caleb and Kody?"

"Kody and Xev."

"Xev . . . the cute, sweet, bashful boy with that lovely accent and extravagant hair?"

He smiled at her kind description of Xev's unorth-odox appearance that had been known to make others scream and cross the street whenever they saw him for the first time. Some had been a lot more cruel, which was why Xev preferred to stay in his cat form, for the most part. He only appeared human around Nick, Kody, and his mom.

Leave it to his mom to not judge Xev on anything other than his character and heart. "That's the one."

"Well, just don't make a mess. Do you need me to do anything for you?"

Stay safe and don't ever get hurt because of me. But he could never say that out loud.

Nick shook his head. "Nah. We're good. You rest." He stepped away from the bed and closed the door before he returned to the living room, where his friends waited.

Kody looked at him expectantly. "Well?"

"She remembers absolutely nothing. Her last memory was when I went to school."

Xev moved to check on the windows and see if the crows were still there. "Where did Livia find her?"

"She wouldn't tell me. Only that she'd overheard

some things she wasn't supposed to, and found her that way."

Kody screwed up her face. "What could she have possibly heard?"

"No idea."

Kody looked at Xev, who in turn shrugged. "I've only spoken to you and Nick." He paused before he spoke again. "And while I don't mean to downplay this matter with your mother . . . I think we might have bigger problems at the moment."

Nick groaned as even more dread filled him. He really was going to give birth to a diamond before all was said and done. "What?"

Xev stepped back and opened the curtains for them to see the dark clouds and clear sill. There was no longer a single bird in sight. "The Memitim are gone. Given our luck, I'll take odds that means they've found Caleb's location, and are currently in the midst of making lunch of him."

CHAPTER 7

Nick would definitely take those odds that Caleb was currently the main course of a Memitim hoedown feast. But he hesitated to go after Caleb, even to protect him, and leave his mother alone again. Unlike Caleb, his mother wasn't a warrior demon. She was human. Completely defenseless in their world.

Could this be another trap?

Kody gently nudged him toward Xev. "Go. Protect Caleb. You know I'd die before I let anyone take your mother. I'll call Simi and get her here. Nothing will get through the two of us. You know that. We are the epitome of the immovable object and unstoppable force in one team."

Only then did he relax and incline his head to her. "You're the best."

"Remember that the next time I annoy you and you want to break up with me."

Laughing, he gave her a quick kiss before he and Xev flashed to Caleb's antebellum mansion.

In the elegant black-and-white marble foyer, they could hear the storm outside, slamming against the windows. Everything was dark and creepy as lightning flashed and crows cawed. Shattered glass and puddles of water littered the floor. The decapitated head of a stone angel statue lay near the wall where it must have landed after being flung through one of the shattered windows and shutters. Its soulless eyes stared at Nick as if accusing him of not being here for the fight.

Where the heck was everyone? It was so incredibly sinister and quiet. He couldn't detect a single living soul inside the house.

Terrified they were too late, Nick took the stairs

two at a time until he was inside Caleb's bedroom. Frowning in sudden confusion, he froze at the doorway and took in the peculiar scene.

Caleb was awake and on his feet. Weak, pale, and shaking, he stood in the corner, holding his ancient demonic battle sword with Livia in front of him. They were alone in the room with the crows dive-bombing the windows, trying to break in, and Caleb egging them on with every bit of stupid bravado only a demon on the verge of collapse could pull off and still sound badass while doing it.

"Thank the gods it's you," Livia said between her ragged breaths. "I thought the Memitim had finally broken through his protection spells. I've been so terrified of what we would do if that happened! Oh, Nick! Once again, you're my hero!"

Xev scowled in distaste of her melodramatic praise as he glanced around the walls that were alight with the ancient oils and symbols Caleb had used to seal off his property from his enemies.

Snarling, Caleb angled his sword at Xev. "What's

he doing here?" His disgusted tone likened Xev to the fecal matter of a dung beetle's tick.

"He came with me to make sure you were all right."

"Yeah, I bet. You sure he didn't tell the Memitim where to find me, and then lead them here just to ensure they didn't get lost on the way over?"

Xev winced at the accusation. Ignoring Caleb, he closed the distance between him and Nick. "I'll—"

"Get out!" Caleb's voice wasn't human as he stepped around Livia. It carried the full weight of his demonic power. "I don't want you here!"

For a moment, Nick thought Caleb's powers had returned, until Caleb tried to blast Xev and nothing happened. Instead, Caleb fell back against the wall, dropped his sword weakly, and slid to the floor.

Gasping, Livia went to him to help him up. "It's okay, Malphas. I won't let anything happen to you. Nothing will get through me."

His expression stricken, Xev sighed as he clapped Nick on the back. "I'll help guard your mother. See to Caleb's safety." He vanished, but not before Nick felt him strengthen the shields around Caleb's house to keep the Memitim at bay.

There was also a mysterious and powerful blast that made the crows shriek and scatter in the storm. One he knew came from Xevikan.

Snorting at Xev's twisted retribution and his insistence on protecting Caleb even though Caleb continued to curse and insult him, Nick went to help Caleb back to bed. "Where's Zavid?"

Livia shook her head. "I don't know. He was gone when I returned."

Weird. It wasn't normal for Zavid to go out on his own. Like Xev, he wasn't exactly a people demon, and he didn't have much more than the most rudimentary understanding of the human world. Modern man baffled him, so he typically avoided all interaction with them like a social plague on his crotch. Gaming was about as close to humanity as he wanted to come.

Even then, he only gamed with Caleb and Nick.

"I'm just glad I got back when I did," Livia said as she tucked the covers around Caleb. "Another minute and I think they'd have penetrated his barrier and had him."

Caleb grimaced as he shifted in the bed. "Where's Kody?"

"She's with my mom."

He grabbed the front of Nick's shirt in a deceptively strong grasp. "Keep her safe."

"That was the plan. I'm not intending to sacrifice her to an ancient god anytime soon."

Nodding, Caleb let go, and passed out with a sigh.

"Wow," Livia said as she covered him with another blanket. "Kody means a lot to him, doesn't she?"

"How do you mean?"

"Just that I've noticed how much care they take of each other. How much time they spend together. Whenever Kody's not with you, she's over here, sequestered with Caleb. Even late at night. They seem to really care about each other. I wish I had someone who cared for me like that. It must be nice."

He'd never really given it much thought, but now that she mentioned it, they were together a lot. And, in spite of his concerns about her possibly betraying them one day, Caleb did watch over Kody with a great deal of concern. . . .

Nick glanced at the bed as a bad feeling went through him.

No. It was a stupid fear. While Caleb could be a serious horn-dog when it came to those of the female persuasion, he tended to go after a specific type of woman who was older and much . . . less wholesome-looking than Kody.

His girl was definitely not Caleb's type. At all. Not even a little.

Besides, neither Caleb nor Kody would ever cheat on him like that.

Would they?

Heck no. Refusing to let that seed be planted in his mind, Nick scowled at Livia. "So what did you want to talk to me about?"

She took his hand and led him from Caleb's room. When she spoke, it was in the lowest of whispers. "I want you to be careful, Malachai. There are so many out to harm you. I don't think you're aware of exactly how many enemies surround you on any given day."

He bit back a laugh. She was definitely wrong about that. "Think I have a pretty good idea."

"Do you?" She gestured at the damage the Memitim had done to Caleb's house. "Then you're aware that Caleb is looking for a way to break free of his service to you?"

Yeah, okay, that one caught him off guard. He'd had no idea. "What?"

She nodded. "I think it's what weakened his protection barrier and allowed them in. He's been summoning stronger powers for some time now in an effort to find someone who can reclaim his soul from you. It could be why he has no powers now. I'm thinking he might have traded them off for it. If you were to die while he's essentially mortal, he'd be freed from what binds him to your bloodline."

Could that be true?

Nick swallowed hard at something that really wasn't all *that* farfetched. Caleb did want his freedom. Even bad enough to die for it. "He didn't tell me that."

"Of course not. Why would he?" Livia bit her lip. "And I could be wrong, but I find it strange that all of this started *after* he supposedly sealed the gates for you, don't you?"

Her dark eyes sad, she shook her head. "You know, if someone were to take you with his help, they could easily free him as a reward. I know Noir or Azura would be eternally grateful, and more than happy to show their appreciation with just such an act."

Nick's frown deepened as he considered what she was saying. Could there be any truth to it?

Would Caleb sell him out?

She sighed heavily. "I'm so sorry, my lord. I don't mean to upset you with such possible truths to consider when everyone lies to you. I know it must be hard."

"How do you mean?"

"Well . . . you know. . . . First, you find out that you're not human. That the woman you thought was your benevolent godmother is a goddess in disguise who hid your birthright and bound your powers from you. Without your permission or knowledge. That your father was never what you thought. Instead of a human criminal, he's a demon hiding amongst them. That he wants you dead, so you won't take his power from him. Then you learn that your friend Caleb isn't a friend in school, but a demon sent by your father to watch over and kill you if necessary before you drain his powers from him and take his place as Malachai. That Nekoda is a girl sent by your enemies to carve out your heart and deliver it to them before you can claim your birthright to fight them, as is your full right. Your own mother kept the real truth of your birth from you. She let you think that she cared for your father, instead of telling you how much she hated him, and what really happened between them. Is there anyone in your life who hasn't lied bitterly to you?"

He winced as she laid bare just how unbelievable his life and conception had been. Truth really was stranger than fiction. If he'd put this in a book or movie, no one would have ever believed it.

Some days, he still didn't.

But she was wrong about one thing. There was always one person he could count on for the truth.

"Bubba," he said defensively.

She arched a brow at that. "You sure?"

Well, he was until she gave him *that* evil look.

Now . . .

"I'm positive." But his tone belied the insecurity she'd created.

She laughed. "You're so sweet and naive. It's what I love best about you."

Yeah, right. *That*, he knew better. "Naive" was a word no one in their right mind could ever apply to Nicholas Ambrosius Aloysius Gautier.

"Please. I was born jaded." With serious trust issues where the world was concerned. No one pulled the wool over his eyes.

A slow, insidious smile curved Livia's lips. "That's what *you* think. But trust me, you're way too innocent for your own good."

"How so?"

"Bubba said he'd never hurt you—that he'd always look out for you, no matter what, and now he's dating your mother. How do you think that'll end? He put his own selfishness above your best interest. Sooner or later, all things come to an end. He will hurt you. You both know that."

Stepping away from Nick, she bit her lip seductively. "When this affair with your mother implodes . . . and it will . . . you won't ever speak to him again. Because it'll be too painful for your mother for you to have a relationship with him. So the only real father you've ever known will be ripped out of your life. Bubba knows that. You know that. Maybe it's what he really wanted. Maybe he wanted you gone and just didn't want to come out and say it."

Those words slammed into Nick. Could there be any truth to that? Could Bubba truly want him out of his life?

Was it possible that he was nothing but a nuisance to the big guy?

"And what about Mark?" she asked. "Do you really think he enjoys playing babysitter to you all the time? They're grown men, Nick. You're just an annoying little kid. And you're not even theirs. You're nothing to them. Just a cling-on they can't get rid of."

He ground his teeth as those words stung him hard. She was right. He'd had those fears in the past, but hadn't wanted to believe them.

Now . . .

"Then there's your boss, Kyrian. The two-thousand-year-old Greek general who hid that truth from you of what he really was. Servant to the goddess Artemis. And don't get me started on the secrets Acheron keeps. He's not just a Dark-Hunter, Nick. Nor an Atlantean. He's an ancient god. Yet he would die before he ever allowed you to know that about himself. And when the day comes and you find out the truth, you will become his worst enemy. He will condemn you to death for your knowledge. And that curse is what will set you down the path you can't divert. That very path you're trying so hard to run from."

A shiver rolled down his spine as she confirmed something about the ancient Atlantean he'd long suspected. Something that Acheron had deflected with great skill anytime Nick had tried to ask about it.

"As I said, you are surrounded by liars you can't trust. People who constantly lie to your face. They all keep massive secrets. Why? Because they're not your friends, in spite of what you think. They don't care about you, Nick. Not really. If they did, they'd tell you everything and keep nothing from you. But they don't want you to be close to them. They don't want you to know them or the truth, because you mean *nothing* where they're concerned. You *are* nothing."

The truth of those words bit him deep inside his heart. But he refused to let her know she'd hit her mark with them. He wasn't the kind of guy to ever give that power to another person. He kept his hurt to himself. Only Kody and his mother were allowed to see his pain. "I need to check on Zavid."

"Someone else who speaks one truth to your face and another behind your back."

"What?" he gasped before he could stop himself. "What does he say?"

"He doesn't trust you, either. He thinks you're weak. A mama's boy who can't tie his shoes without her help. He pities you."

Offended, Nick glared at Livia. So much for keeping his emotions in. But this . . . this had blindsided him.

He'd had no idea that Zavid had felt that way, especially since Nick had saved his life.

"I'm not the one who said it." She blinked at him innocently. "I'm just telling you this for your own good. You should know how they really feel. What they say when you're not around. I would never treat you that way. I think too much of you to do that."

Biting her lip, she stepped closer to him. "I know what it's like to be alone and to have no one to trust. To have nowhere to turn." She stood on her toes to kiss him.

Nick stepped back before their lips met. While Livia was a very attractive female, she wasn't the kind of girl he was interested in and he'd never hurt Kody like that. He wasn't that kind of guy and he had no intention of ever being that type of slime ball. Hearts were sacred things and when someone entrusted theirs to you, it was your duty to keep faith. Nick had no intention of breaking his honor for anything. "I need to find out why Zavid left Caleb alone."

"Malachai!"

He ignored her call and kept going. Every molecule of his body told him to put as much distance as he could between them, as quickly as possible.

For once he listened. He had to think through this without hearing her voice in his head, alongside the ones that told him how worthless he was.

Nick ran the rest of the way down the stairs and out the door, looking for Zavid. The moment his feet hit the street outside the protected barrier, the Memitim attacked like screaming, love-sick fangirls all over their latest fixation.

Cursing, he threw his hand up and zapped them away from him. "Demons, please! I ain't your hellmonkey. Really don't have time for this!"

The one nearest him had the nerve to hiss like a cat. "The Malachai protects Malphas? Why? We served you well. And here you dare to side with our enemy after he betrayed us all? How could you?"

Nick was aghast at his fury. "First, you didn't serve *me*. You fought for some ancestor I don't even know the name of. Dude, for real? Put that card back in the deck. It ain't gonna win this round. Second, Caleb fell in love and walked away from that war you're talking about. Who can blame him for that? You're the ones who came at him when you should have just left him in peace to live with his wife and be happy. If you didn't want him to kick your butts, you should have stayed at home. That's on you. Not him."

The leader Memitim cawed loudly. "He knew our secrets to betray them to our enemies. We could not suffer him to live with such knowledge when he could destroy us."

"And you knew his. . . . Assured mutual destruction. Again, you could have chosen to leave him alone. Yet you didn't. Fair's fair. You came at him. He defeated you. Now grow a set and deal. Let him be."

They rose up again into a dark cyclone to attack Caleb's barrier. But at least they were no longer after him.

Nick wasn't sure if he should be happy or not.

Weary and sick, he sighed at their stubborn determination. "Do I have to banish you back to whatever hole you crawled out of? For real? This is what you want to do with your freedom?"

Their answer was to continue their assault. So, yeah. This was what they wanted to do with their new-found lives.

It made no sense to him whatsoever. Why would they continue down this path when they could do something positive or constructive?

Like get a beignet. Grab some coffee.

Get a girl and have some happy private adult fun time.

Why choose death when they could choose life? Weren't there girl raven-demons for them to pursue? Really?

Stunned at the waste, Nick stood back in the storm to watch them as they flew in wave after wave against Caleb's protection barrier. He wasn't sure if he should be appalled or impressed by their raw, single-minded determination.

It also said a lot about Caleb's power that it could hold even while he was drained. Still . . . he felt bad for both sides. The Memitim for not being able to let it go after all these centuries, and Caleb for not being able to move on because of their obstinacy.

Why dwell on the past when you have a perfectly good tomorrow to look forward to screwing up? Mark's favorite saying went through his head. There was definitely something to be said for that. Especially while watching them pursue their madness. They were so focused on Caleb that they'd destroyed themselves trying to strike at him.

Was it worth it?

Definitely not.

Gah, I hope I'm never that *stupid. 'Cause let's face it. I basically hog all the dumb, most days.*

But there was nothing he could do to help them with their idiocy today. And right now, he had a renegade demon who might be neck-deep in trouble and needing his help to locate. A mom to guard. Funky weather to avoid.

And a strange mystery to solve.

He stared at the Memitim. *How do I get rid of those?* And again, he had that off, hollow feeling in his gut that something wasn't right.

That his time was running out.

All of a sudden, the Memitim scattered as if terrified. Yeah, that had to be a really bad sign.

Nick cringed at the omen as more lightning flashed,

narrowly missing him. That was stunning, but not as much as the beautiful teenaged girl who stepped out of it and eyed him with great curiosity.

Completely dry in spite of the weather, she had rich caramel skin with dark hair that fell in intricate braids around a perfect face. But it wasn't her beauty that made his senses stir, it was the amount of power that emanated from her. This was a preter of unparalleled Source power. If she announced herself to him as Azura, he wouldn't be surprised.

Her powers were *that* strong.

Dressed in a short skirt and a halter, she met his stunned expression with a shrug as she approached him with a slow, seductive walk. "You wanted them gone. They're gone now."

Yeah, but he wasn't quite sure he should be thanking her for it. Or running in the opposite direction and screaming like a kindergartener on Benadryl who'd just met Freddy Krueger.

His gut voted for the boogeyman bolt.

"Who are you?"

She smiled. "Don't you know?"

"Not a clue."

She paused beside him to sniff at his shoulder and hair. Kind of creepy. Yeah, he was leaning even more toward the boogeyman scenario. "*You* are the Malachai?"

Nick hesitated at her tone that was almost insulting. Even so, when a being this powerful asked that question, it was never a good idea to give a straight answer. "Uh . . . Malamaybe?"

Cupping his face, she pressed her cheek to his and took a deep breath. "You are *not* Monakribos." That was the name of the first Malachai, who'd been cursed . . . she must know a lot about his kind to have the given name of his ancestor. Most had no clue about that.

Or, like Xev and Caleb, she was older than dirt.

"I'm . . ." Nick hesitated. Technically, he was the Ambrose Malachai, but he was superstitious about taking that name yet. Even though it was correct, it just seemed like a really bad idea to call down that kind of mojo right now. The longer he could keep from becoming the monster he was destined to be, the better. "Nick."

Pulling back, she curled her lip. "That's a stupid name for a Malachai. What fool named you?"

"Excuse me? My mother is a wonderful lady."

Her brow shot up and Nick remembered too late that Malachais were supposed to hate their mothers. Not defend them.

"You still haven't told me who you are."

Cocking her head, she studied him with a scowl. "How can a Malachai so powerful not know me on sight?"

Maybe because he still hadn't quite mastered all of his powers? But again, he wasn't about to own up to that when dealing with someone who could mop the street with him.

"Are you Yrre?" It seemed the most reasonable guess that she'd be the rider who'd almost mowed him down in school. It made sense. They were both dressed in white, came out of nowhere, and left him totally baffled.

She shook her head and laughed. "Do I look like that cow-faced dog?"

Uh, no. She looked pretty hot, actually. Hot

enough to get him into serious trouble if Kody caught her standing this tight to his personal space.

Nick stepped back.

She followed. With an adoring expression, she brushed her hand through his hair. "Do you not feel your connection to me?"

He only felt a traitorous part of his body that wanted to be connected to her. But he knew better than to listen to that part of himself. It had a mind of its own that could get him into all kinds of nightmares if he let it. "Not sure what you mean."

"Yes, you do. You know exactly of what I speak. You feel the blood that tells you who I am."

"Nope. I feel nothing." Except the urge to get away from her before she got him into all kinds of trouble no amount of apologizing could get him out of—not even a shiny object from Jared's. He'd meant what he said. He would never, ever break Kody's trust or her heart.

Not intentionally.

Nick froze mid-step as a peculiar image went through his mind. He saw the girl in ancient armor, wrapped around a multiheaded dragon. An inherited memory that came from one of his Malachai predecessors. In that instant, he knew the goddess's name. "Tiamat."

She inclined her head to him. "See, you do know me."

Sort of. And one thing he knew about her . . . "You're supposed to be dead."

Her laughter rang like music in his ears. "No one can kill something as powerful as I. You only change my state of being. So why have you summoned me from my slumber, Malachai?"

A chill went down his spine at that question. "I didn't summon you."

Scowling, she gently fingered his cheek. "It's always about you, Malachai. Haven't you learned that yet? Besides, who else would dare disturb me?"

"Someone with a death wish?"

She laughed aloud at that. "You're a cheeky one, aren't you?"

Not at the moment. At the moment, though, it pained him to admit it even to himself, he was rather afraid. This was one of the most dangerous of the chaos gods. She had birthed more monsters than Echidna.

Come to think of it, she might have even birthed Echidna. He never could keep all that mythology straight.

Lowering her head, she stepped back as if she was listening to the aether voices that constantly drove Nick crazy whenever he tried to understand them. Her eyes glowed a deep, scary red. She dropped her hand from his face. "As much as I would love to stay and chat, I have much to do and little time to work it."

Before he could blink, she was gone.

Rain poured down over him as soon as she was gone. Crap. He had a bad, bad feeling deep in the pit of his stomach.

Suddenly, everything around him stopped. Even the rain. No. Not stopped. It froze in place like a painting. Nick turned a slow circle as he tried to make sense of what was happening.

He felt so out of sync with everything. Out of time. It was like being in the Nether Realm or the darkness that existed between dimensions. Only he wasn't lost or misplaced. He was in his time and correct plane.

Just not lined up right.

Like a cog that was ever so slightly misaligned. And then he felt it . . . that presence that had been missing for so long. "Ambrose?"

"Find the Eye." It was the faintest of whispers.

"What? What eye?"

"The Eye of Ananke." Ambrose appeared to him as nothing more than a mere translucent shadow with red eyes. The only way he knew for a fact it was him was the faint outline of Artemis's double bow-and-arrow mark on his cheek. It marked the spot where the Greek goddess would one day remove his soul from him.

That familiar red demonic gaze burned into Nick. "I shouldn't have tried to reset the past. We were born a damned abomination that should never have been conceived."

His breathing labored, Ambrose fell to his knees on the sidewalk beside him. He looked up with an expression of woeful abandon. "Listen to me, Nick. You have to find the Eye and follow your true course. The one we were meant to follow before I screwed up so badly. Fast! It's the only hope we have. You have to stay true to our original course. Trust me on this. Please! Do not stray from our path!"

For a moment, his eyes turned to the shade of blue Nick saw reflected in a mirror whenever he gazed in one. "Of all the mistakes I've made, the one I regret most is robbing you of the years where you were able to dream of normality. At your age, I knew nothing of Kyrian's world. Of Dark-Hunters, ancient gods, and Were-Hunters. I was just a stupid kid, with stupid kid dreams." He laughed bitterly. "I thought I was going to be a fancy uptown lawyer. That I'd have a wife and kids . . ." His eyes returned to red. "I'm so sorry I took that from you. I just wanted to save us. Give us something to hope for."

"Wide is the gate that leads to destruction," Nick said, quoting his mother's favorite saying, "and many are those who enter through it. But the gate is narrow and the way is straight that leads to life, and few are those who find it."

Ambrose snorted. "It's why there's a highway to hell, but only a single stairway to heaven." He looked up at Nick. "I've lost the war. By fighting, I only made it worse. Find the Eye and reset our course. We have to go back in order to move forward. It's the only hope we have. The Riders are out and they are about to take you down, little brother. Move fast, with purpose, or we're both lost. There's so much you have to do, that I can't even begin to tell you how to fix it. But the Eye can." He rose slowly to his feet. "I won't be able to help after this. You're on your own."

Nick gave a short half laugh. "I'm good with that. I came into this world alone, and that's how I'll leave it. . . . I was born standing up and talking back. Cajun proud and Cajun strong from my first breath to my last."

Wings shot out of Ambrose's back as he changed from human to full Malachai form. His skin marbled red and black as his eyes turned to full-on pret. Fangs and claws flashing, he grabbed Nick's jaw in his fist and tilted his head until they locked gazes. "We are Malachai above all else. Now and forever. Never forget that." Throwing his head back, he let loose a horrific blast of blue-tinged fire toward the sky before he vanished.

Shaken and trembling, Nick stood there as everything returned to normal and the rain again saturated him. But in his mind, he saw what Ambrose did. Nick saw the bloody future that awaited them, and there in the cold, winter rain, he refused to be intimidated. He refused to allow fate and Ambrose to win.

I will not become you, old man.

He would find this Eye and figure out where Ambrose and the others had gone wrong. He would stop whatever hell-monkey was currently loose and messing with his friends and family.

But most of all, he would make sure that he never fulfilled the destiny that said he would destroy this world. Kody believed in the prophecy that said he was the Malachai who would save their line. And he believed in her.

Since the day he was born, he'd been defying the odds. Today was not the day to stop that trend. Unlike Ambrose, he wasn't about to give up or give in.

So long as there was breath in his body, there was life. So long as there was life, there was hope. And so long as there was hope, there was the possibility of victory.

Life wasn't about just getting by. It was about getting through, no matter what, and making the most of every minute.

A chill went down his spine as he remembered what his father had said to him. *The Malachai will never be forgotten. But it's entirely up to you as to how you'll be remembered.*

Nick Gautier would not be remembered as a coward or a villain. He was going out a hero and a champion.

And he would not go down without a vicious, vicious fight.

As he started after Zavid, his phone rang. It was Kody. He answered immediately. "Hey, *cher.* What's up?"

"Where are you?"

"Outside Caleb's. Why? What'cha need?"

"You. Fast as possible. There's something here and it's after your mother."

CHAPTER 8

The instant Nick appeared in his living room, he was violently lifted off his feet and slammed so hard onto the wood floor that it knocked the breath out of him. Flat on his back, he moaned out loud while his ears rang violently. Ah, dang, it hurt! All he could do was choke and wheeze. It felt like he'd been mowed down by an eighteen-wheeler traveling faster than the speed of sound.

Or tackled by Bubba for prematurely interrupting an episode of *Oprah*.

Someone, grab me an inhaler and shove it in my mouth. Yeah, okay, he wasn't asthmatic, but he was willing to learn and at this point, he definitely felt that bronchial burn.

"Oh no! Akri-Nicky! You okay? The Simi didn't know it was her favorite blue-eyed demon boy when she hit him so hard so as to protect his precious akramama. Oh no!" Simi leaned over him with her red-and-black pigtails framing her adorable face as she slapped at his cheeks to revive him. "You still living and breathing and not broken? 'Cause if you not, can the Simi eat your dead, meaty remains? Please, please, please? Maybe some of them bones, too, 'cause the marrow can be quite tasty in its own right."

Now, to a normal person, that might seem like an odd request. But to those a little behind on the schematics, there really wasn't anything normal about Nick's life or those in it. Being a Charonte demon, Simi had a fondness for human meat, but luckily for humanity, she wasn't allowed to chow down on it without express permission of either the donor or her father. Which her main akri tended not to give her.

Thank goodness for that.

Nick stared up into her bright, friendly eyes. For

all her bloodthirsty cravings, she was quite adorable, and loyal to a scary fault. Like a fluffy killer attack bunny.

Dressed in a short black-and-white skull tank dress, she wore a rose-lace hoodie over it. Her red-and-black-striped leggings matched her hair and she had on a pair of black and red floral Doc Martens.

"Sadly for you, I think I'm going to live, Simi," he choked out with a wheeze. "You can stop slapping me now. I've already lost enough sense. Can't afford to lose any more brain cells. I really really need my last three before I forget how to spell my name. It's hard enough to pronounce."

"Well, poo." She sat back with an adorable pout. "Not poo that you'll live, 'cause the Simi would probably miss you if you died, but poo that I'll miss all that good old salty boy meat." She poked at his ribs. "Though we needs be fattening you up some to make you really good eats. Hmmm." She licked her lips as if imagining what he'd taste like basted in barbecue sauce—Simi's prime condiment of choice.

Yeah. Okay. Not wanting to think about that, Nick

pushed himself up to face Xev with a grimace. "Y'all could have warned me about the attack Simi you had on door duty."

Xev shrugged nonchalantly. "I wasn't completely sure it was you. Besides, she was a lot more gentle in her attack on you than I'd have been." He swept a bitterly amused glance over Nick's body. "With her, you're still in one piece. So stop whining like a baby before I have Simi burp you."

Crossing his arms over his chest, Xev inclined his head toward the bedroom. "Kody's with your mother, who's unconscious for some unknown reason. No matter what we try, we can't seem to get Cherise to wake up again."

"Could it be Tiamat? I saw her just before I came here."

Xev went so still that for a moment, Nick thought everything had frozen again.

Until Xev blinked ever so slowly. "Nyria?"

Her features completely ashen, Kody came out of the room. "What did you call me?"

He ignored her question. "Tiamat is free."

The color drained from her face, too. "What?" She looked to Nick for confirmation. "Are you sure?"

Nick nodded. "She was at Caleb's. She thought I'd summoned her."

"Did you?"

Should he be offended by the way she asked that? A part of him thought so, given that only an outright moron would do something *that* stupid. And while he'd been known to pull some award-winning acts of dumb, he'd never been quite that asleep at the wheel.

At least, not yet, that he knew of.

"I don't make it a habit of summoning gods I don't know, no offense. Especially not one I've never heard of before. I don't even play those video games after what happened with Madaug. How slow on the uptake do I look, and don't answer that. I have a very fragile male ego where you're concerned." Nick scowled as Xev carried his unconscious mother out of the bedroom and placed her on the couch, between them. "What are *you* doing, champ?"

"I am not letting her out of our sight. I will not be

blamed for her harm, and I will allow no harm to come to her while she's in my custody." Xev placed a small round pillow beneath her head, then covered her with the pink crocheted blanket she kept tossed over the back of the couch, and took up a post at her feet, facing her with his right hand on her leg.

Okie-dokie, he was just a *little* paranoid.

And in that moment, the full weight of Xev's true trauma hit Nick. The ancient ex-god was in the middle of an all-out panic attack. A bad one, too, by the looks of it. Kind of like Nick whenever his chemistry teacher sprang a pop quiz on him at school.

"Xev?"

He didn't hear him. His breathing labored, he wasn't really with them. Instead, he appeared to be in a waking nightmare of some kind.

Nick exchanged a concerned look with Kody before he closed the distance between him and Xev. "Xevikan!" Still, he didn't respond as he kept looking around as if seeking an unseen attacker.

Or several thousand of them.

Pulling Xev's hand from his mother's leg, Nick

forced him to take a step back. "Daraxerxes!" Gah, he hoped he pronounced that name right.

Only then did Xev focus on Nick's face. But he still wasn't completely recovered.

"They're coming." His voice was firm and intense. "We have to secure the children and women. They'll hit where we're weakest. You stay here with the others. I have to get to Lil and warn her. She'll be their first target. If they reach her first, they can neutralize Caleb's forces and crash the gates."

Nick winced at the anguish in his voice. Lil would have been Caleb's wife. Lilliana. The one Caleb blamed Xev for allowing to die. But from those words and the way Xev was acting, it didn't sound like Xev had betrayed him and led the enemies inside the gate to take them out. More like he'd done his best to keep her safe.

"Xevikan!" he tried again.

Flinching, Xev turned as one of the symbols on the wall lit up. Recognition widened his eyes before they darkened with the bitterest hatred. He hissed like a cat and backed away from it.

Kody approached him slowly. "Xev?" Gingerly, she touched his chest. "Are you with us?"

His breathing still labored, he covered her hand with his and held it as if she were as precious to him as she was to Nick. A tic started in his jaw before he gave a slow nod. "You feel that?"

"Feel what?" Kody asked.

He looked to Simi. "Charonte?"

"Cursed god?" she shot back in irritation.

Xev rolled his eyes before he went to the door to take a defensive position behind the hinges. He man- ifested fireballs around his hands as someone knocked on it.

Nick scowled. "You know, X, from my experience, the bad guys don't usually knock."

A snide smile curved his lips. "They do when their brand of evil has to be invited in in order to enter."

And now his gut was back to producing diamonds. Xev had a very valid point with that. There were Daimons and certain other entities who definitely required specific invitations into domiciles to wreak havoc and harm. Nick really wished he lived a life where he didn't have to know that.

Great. Just great. More nightmares to worry about.

Hoping for the best, Nick went to the peephole to glance out, then passed a droll stare to Xev. "Put away your paranoia. It's just my godmother. No doubt, the police contacted her about the attack on my mom, and she wanted to check on us. She's barely five feet tall, and ninety pounds soaking wet. I don't think we have anything to fear. And she's probably terrified. Last thing she needs is for you to give her a heart attack."

Unlocking the door, he opened it and pulled the tiny Creole midwife who'd helped bring him into the world into his arms for a tight hug. "Hey, Aunt Mennie."

She squeezed him back while her sisterlocks tickled his nose. "Hey, Boo. I hope you don't mind. But given all the weirdness I wanted to come by and check on you and your . . ." Her voice trailed off as her gaze went past his shoulder to Xev. Instantly bug-eyed, she gasped audibly.

Not thinking anything about her reaction, since most people tended to greet Xev like a cross between a leper and Bigfoot's bigger and nastier older brother who was jacked up on steroids, Nick shut the door. "Menyara, this is—"

"We know each other, don't we, Cam?" Xev's voice was so cold, they could have used it to flash-freeze helium popsicles on the Pontchartrain Bridge in August.

Menyara staggered back and would have fallen had Nick not been there to catch her.

"Mennie? Are you all right?"

"What have you done, Nick?" she breathed in a horrified tone as she continued to stare at Xev as if he was the devil incarnate. "What have you done?" she repeated.

Xev glared at her. "Interesting that you would blame *him*, when this all started with you and *your* siblings."

Shaking her head, Menyara dragged her gaze to each of them in turn—Xev, Simi, Kody, Cherise, and Nick—before she closed her eyes. "Who unlocked

Nick's powers? For the love of the Source, why would you do such a thing? Have you any idea what you've done?"

Sheepish, Kody bit her lip before she explained their actions. "We had no choice. Nick's ousia had been split from his body by his enemies who wanted to weaken him enough to kill him. It was the only way to save him and return him to this dimension and save his life. Had we not moved fast, he'd be dead now."

Menyara let out a weary sigh as she sat down on the armchair and hung her head in her hands. "You should have come to me before you acted."

"I tried. I really did." Kody started forward, but Xev stopped her.

When he spoke again, his tone was like that of a patient parent to a beloved child. "This isn't on you, little one. This started long before you were sent here to kill Nick. Long before you were recruited to your cause. Don't let her put her sins on your innocent shoulders."

His eyes flashing bright red, Xev curled a furious lip as he neared Menyara. "How could you do such a thing to *them*? Have you learned nothing over the centuries about tampering with human fate and free will? About playing with lives when you should leave well enough alone?"

Looking up, Menyara met his gaze without flinching. "We had *no* choice. You've no idea how powerful Adarian had grown. How incredibly dangerous he was to everyone and everything he came into contact with."

"And whose fault was that?"

She ignored his question. "We couldn't control him anymore. He'd been unleashed on this world. An unstoppable monster. We had no other way of even finding him. Everything we tried, failed. He was becoming such a threat that at any moment, he could have come for us and won. Torn out our throats and laughed about it as he drank our blood from his own fists. It was our only hope of fighting him. The only way we could think to even slow him down long enough to put him back in chains."

"By making his powers stronger? Who thought *that* was a good idea?"

"It was meant to negate his powers."

Xev scoffed angrily. "You had no right to involve an innocent life without telling her what you were doing! Without asking her permission!" He paced the floor like a caged beast looking for a way to attack its taunter, who in this case appeared to be Menyara.

"We had every right to do whatever it took to protect all the innocents of this world. One sacrifice for millions of others. It was an equitable exchange."

Still, Xev denied her logic and clung to his steadfast argument. "It wasn't your place to make that call."

She ignored his fury. "Mankind couldn't stand against the ušumgallu centuries ago when they knew about them and were prepared to fight them. Now . . . they're completely helpless against the Malachai and his allies. They don't even know of them. Never mind raise an army to fight him, or use magic and the elements to bind him! What would you have had us do? Stand aside and watch all of you mow the humans down for your sick pleasure?"

Slack-jawed, Xev froze in response to her question as if he'd just realized something. His breathing labored, he met Menyara's furious glower. "Her father isn't Verlyn. He can't be. I would have sensed it instantly were we siblings."

"No. Azura keeps him sterile for fear he will father a child who can kill or enslave her."

"Rezar?"

"Has been missing for centuries. No one knows what happened to him."

Absolute horror washed over his face as he turned toward Nick. He looked at him as if he'd never seen him before. As if he was looking at him through new eyes.

His gaze fell to Nick's mother and for a moment, Nick thought Xev might actually kill Menyara.

Or toss his cookies.

"You chose a warrior of light for the task." It was a flat, whispered statement, not a question.

"There was no one else. We needed a father born directly from the Kalosum Source powers. He was the closest to them who could still father a daughter for the cause."

Biting his lip, Xev winced. "They're people, not disposable pawns for your selfish games, Cam."

She glared at him. "No one knows that better than I. Everything I've ever done was for the protection of others. For the protection and benefit, and my love of this world, and all those who dwell in it. *I* was the one who stayed here in this hole, to watch over and protect. To be here every step of the way. For them all."

And still Xev's gaze condemned her for her actions. "Does he even know he's a father?"

"Of course not. It would have been a disaster on multiple levels had he ever learned the truth. His daughter was conceived, delivered, and raised under the guise of a completely normal, orphaned human, and appears so to all. No one has ever suspected that she is more than she seems. She never even knew she was an adopted orphan. For all she knows, her adoptive parents are the ones who birthed her."

Xev laughed bitterly. "And yet you did it without his knowledge or consent. You broke every supreme law we once lived by. Used him and her mother. Did the mother *ever* know? Did *any* of them?"

"No. We couldn't afford for them to have any idea. They could have tipped off Adarian if they had. The mother met him one time . . . in a bar, and took him home. As far as she knew, he was a human, just passing through her town for the night."

He cursed her under his breath. "How very typical of you all. You put them in the line of fire without warning or defense. Without full knowledge or understanding. How could you?"

Nick whistled, interrupting them. "Hello? Who here has the faintest clue what they're talking about?"

Not even Simi held her hand up, which said it all. Simi usually knew everything.

But for once, she simply shrugged.

Nick turned his attention back to the only two who did.

Menyara and Xev.

"All right. In that case, could one of you catch the room up? Please? Especially since this seems to be my life and family you're discussing? And I have a really bad feeling about this?"

"You should." Xev crossed his arms over his chest as he continued to glare at Menyara. "Your conception and birth were no accident, Nick. Your entire existence was a trap set for your father."

That had better be a joke. "Excuse me?"

Nodding slowly, Xev turned to face him. "It's what makes you so powerful and dangerous, and sets you apart from all the Malachais who've come before you. You're not just born of the Mavromino. Like the very first Malachai who started this, you, too, through your mother, carry the blood of a Sephiroth warrior."

Those words hit Nick like a fist to his gut. "Excuse me?"

Kody sucked her breath in audibly as Simi gaped so wide, she exposed her fangs.

"It's what gives us hope for him." Menyara stood to face Nick. Wringing her hands, she swallowed hard. "But it wasn't supposed to happen like it did. None of it."

Fret knitted her brow as Menyara tried to explain it to them. "You have to understand, child. We never meant to hurt you or your mother. That wasn't our intent. We only meant to curb Adarian's powers. To leash his anger and fulfill a prophecy that was given to us long ago."

Stunned breathless, Nick exchanged a frown with Simi as he took Kody's hand. Just knowing she was there kept him anchored and grounded as he struggled to come to terms with what Menyara was trying to tell him. Part of him had always suspected this truth, but the other part was angry and hurt. "I'm so confused."

"The Simi bewildered, too. I done gots lost around the block a whiles ago."

Xev laughed bitterly as he spread his arms out and braced his hands on the couch to lean against it. His eyes turned a bright, flaming red as they blazed hot with his own anger and hatred. "It's what they've done to us since the dawn of time, Nick. We who are born of darkness are creatures of great power. Tiamat. Braith. Caleb. Me. You. Your father. The list goes on *infinitās*. It is hatred, pain, bitterness, and rage that feeds our strength. Adversity is the stone on which we hone our swords for battle. What breaks lesser beings and sends them sniveling to their graves fuels us to victory. The cruelty of others doesn't faze us even a little. It's all we know. It is why we are invincible. Why they," he jerked his chin toward Menyara, "can't stand toe-to-toe in battle with us. And they know it. So they break us with the one thing we have no defense against." His gaze went to Kody and then to their locked hands.

Nick frowned. "I don't understand."

Xev swallowed hard before he spoke again. "Because of who we are and how we are born and raised, we tell ourselves that we need nothing. We want nothing. We *are* nothing. That we are despised creatures of darkness. And that's okay by us. We don't need or want the approval or acceptance of *them*." His gaze fell to the floor at Kody's feet. "But there is one thing that will always draw us out against our will, and make us weak."

"The light," Kody breathed.

He gave a subtle nod. "No one will ever take us in battle. We know how to fight against all odds. How to stand strong in any maelstrom. We know how to deal with insults. Cruelty. And viciousness. That *is* and will always be our mother's milk."

Xev gestured toward Nick's unconscious mother. "Sadly, it's unexpected kindness that disarms us. A simple smile that throws us completely off guard. Innocent love that renders us defenseless and sends us to our knees. That's how they cripple and defeat us. Not with war. But with friendship."

Kody shook her head. "Love is never a weakness."

He laughed cruelly. "Your own mother would be the first to violently disagree with that statement, Nyria." His gaze went to Nick. "It's what killed *your* father, Malachai. It's what enslaved me and Caleb to our enemies, and it's what will kill us all in the end."

Menyara snorted rudely. "How dare you speak to them of love when you know nothing of it."

He twisted his lips into the cruel mockery of a smile. "Yes, I had all of you to thank for that, didn't I, Cam? You were all so kind and understanding of me when I was a boy, needing comfort and finding only the coldness of your rebuffs at best . . . the backs of your hands at worst. Your harsh brutality tutored me well on the subject, until all I knew was the hatred that filled me full from tip to root."

Guilt darkened her eyes before she looked away from Xev. "How could we ever trust you? You were suckled by evil incarnate."

"Actually, my wet nurse was a she-fox warrior demon, who took pity on me when no one else would. Or so I'm told. My mother couldn't be bothered with my needs or feeding, as she couldn't have cared less if I lived or died once my father told her I should be left out to the elements, for he, a shining bastion of all-good and light, had no intention of ever claiming me as his son."

He met Nick's gaze. "By the way, I lied earlier when I told you why I fought for the side I did. It wasn't to anger my mother. I truly never cared what she thought of me, one way or another. I betrayed the Malachai and my mother, and fought for the Kalosum, solely to keep faith with my wife. She was the only being I would never in my life disappoint. The only one I would bleed or die for."

Menyara sneered at him. "You're lying! You never had a wife."

But the anguish in his red-tinged, rust-colored eyes

said that Xev spoke from his heart. No, that wasn't a lie. Even though Xev had told Nick himself that he'd never known love, Nick knew that look. Every instinct he possessed told him that Xev was being honest with him, right now. That was the same exact light Caleb had in his eyes whenever he spoke of his Lilliana.

The same expression Kyrian had with Theone. Bubba with Melissa.

That was true love. The kind people wrote sonnets and songs about. The kind that broke your heart and left it shattered for eternity.

"What was her name?" Nick asked.

Xev didn't pause or hesitate with his answer. And when he spoke, his voice softened with reverence, adding further proof that he was telling the truth. "Myone."

Menyara shot to her feet. "Liar! Myone would have *never* had anything to do with one such as *you*! She was one of the purest souls I've ever known." Her anger made Nick wonder who Myone was, but this wasn't the time to ask.

Xev met Menyara's gaze without flinching or backing down. "Do not dishonor her memory by speaking her name with your tainted tongue when you know *nothing* of her true beauty or character! You're just as delusional and hypocritical as my father. You think because you are born of light that you're somehow better and kinder than those who aren't, but you're not. It merely makes you more sanctimonious in your cruelty. Makes you feel entitled in your wrongful actions against others. But you're no better than my mother. If anything, you're worse, because you think your viciousness is justified against us."

He drew a ragged breath, and turned back toward Simi, Kody, and Nick. "And that's why my wife and I had to keep our marriage a secret. Why we had to deny we ever had any kind of relationship at all, and why I had to let her go after only six months, to protect her from my enemies, including my own mother and father, who would have killed her to get back at me. They would never have left us in peace, never allowed her to retain her place of honor. Even though she would have never done anything to betray the Kalosum. None of them would have believed it. I couldn't afford for anyone to know that she held my heart. That I even had one. Good or bad. Light or dark. It mattered not. Had anyone ever learned the truth, we would have been destroyed. Just as Caleb was for daring to hope for a better life with his Lilliana. Just as Adarian was for loving you and your mother. For hoping Cherise could somehow see something more in him besides the monster he'd been born. Like us, he was a pathetic moth dragged against his will to a sweet, vibrant light he couldn't resist or understand. But one he knew he needed in order to live and feel warm."

His gaze dropped to where Nick's hand was wrapped around Kody's. "They beguile us so with their precious ways. And for a moment's worth of warmth in a lifetime of coldness, we are burned and extinguished. Pathetic creatures from our cradles to our graves." He laughed bitterly. "We are ever helpless against them."

For a full minute, Nick couldn't breathe as those bitter, heartfelt words and their implication hit him hard. Could it possibly be true?

Could his mother truly be that innocent orphan

who'd been conceived and sent by the Kalosum for no other purpose than to trap his father?

"Mennie? Tell me you didn't do that to my mom."

Closing her eyes, she turned her face away from him, letting him know that Xev was telling him the truth.

Shattered by the revelations, Nick stepped away from Kody and Simi to approach the woman who'd helped bring him into this world. A woman he'd thought he could always trust. One who'd always promised him that she would never lie or be dishonest.

Not for anything.

When everyone else had turned their back on him and his mom, Menyara had always been there for them. She'd said it was because taking them in like family and helping them was the right thing to do. That she couldn't turn her back on them like everyone else and let them suffer. Not when they needed help.

But she'd left out some seriously vital details.

Sick to his stomach, Nick was quickly learning that Livia had been right. Everyone in his life had lied badly to him. Menyara had kept much, much more from him than just the secret of his father and birth.

She'd hidden her real identity from them. Her real role in both their lives.

His gaze went to his mother and he felt as sick as Caleb had been at school.

How could Menyara do this to her? His mother had no idea she was adopted and had no idea who her real parents were. For that matter, he didn't really know, other than her father was a Sephiroth. That knowledge would kill her. She'd never, ever believe him if he tried to tell her.

His head reeling, he scowled at Menyara. "Who's my real grandmother?"

"It doesn't matter. She died three days after she gave your mother up for adoption, in a car wreck. As did your real grandfather, supposedly in another wreck before the birth. It's why the Gautiers never told her she was adopted. Why bother? With both birth parents dead, there was no reason to ever let Cherise know the truth. For all intents and purposes, the Gautiers are your grandparents. That's all you and your mother ever need to know. The truth would only hurt her."

Maybe, but he was leaning toward Xev with this. His mother had a right to know. And it explained why her parents had been so quick to toss her out when she'd become pregnant as a teenager. The fact that her parents had thrown her away like garbage had played a number on his mother's head. If she knew they weren't really her birth parents, that might make this better.

But then again, it might not. If she found out the truth, she'd have two sets of parents who'd given her up. That might be a lot worse in her mind.

Yeah, life was ever complicated. Ambrose had taught him that. And people didn't always react the way you expected them to. As Acheron so often said, emotions didn't have brains.

And right now, his emotions were all over the place and were definitely not thinking clearly as he tried to make sense of all this.

Which led him back to one other thing he wanted to clarify while Menyara felt the need to come clean with her lies. "Are you really the goddess Cam?"

She nodded.

Cam had been one of the original six primal gods who'd started the first great war of the immortals. A war that had almost ended the world and mankind. She and her siblings had been the ones who'd called for Nick's race to be put down like rabid dogs. All except his one ancestor.

One cursed Malachai.

One cursed Sephiroth.

Tied together for eternity and doomed to fight one last battle that would eventually end the world.

Now, if what Xev said was true, Mennie had used that last Sephiroth to impregnate Nick's grandmother and birth his own mother as a trap for his father, knowing his father wouldn't be able to resist her. Cherise was the yin to Adarian's yang. An innocent human with the blood of a Sephiroth. A human who had no knowledge of the inhuman creatures who shared this world with mankind.

Unable to believe it, Nick glanced from Menyara to his mother. "You set my mother up?"

"I'm so sorry, Nicholas."

Stunned, he struggled to breathe as he again had that feeling of being out of sync with time. Of everything slowing down. "Is that why she's so pure of heart? So incorruptible and unwilling to believe in anything supernatural?"

Mennie nodded. "For some reason, she can't see it and has an unreasonable reaction to it whenever we try to explain it to her. I tried to hint about it once when she was a girl and she reacted so violently that I erased it from her memory, and have kept her from anything to do with it ever since. She simply can't handle it."

Now he understood why his mother had reacted so badly when Ambrose had tried to tell her the truth about the paranormal world around them. It must have triggered something inside her that had been unable to deal with the fact that she wasn't completely human. That she'd literally been so ill-conceived.

Ambrose must not have ever experienced this moment where he learned the truth about her birth and his heritage.

And maybe that was why his mother was unconscious now. Because she was part Sephiroth, whatever was infecting Caleb might be infecting her, too.

Menyara sighed before she spoke again. "It's also why Cherise is incapable of seeing the evil in others. Why she's like a beacon that calls out to so many who need kindness. Acheron. Caleb. Kyrian. The Peltiers. Like all Sephirii, she's innately soothing and gentle to be around. A spiritual balm. Unless they're in battle and are defending what they love, the Sephirii can calm the most restless of souls."

And that made him furious. Because of what they'd done to her, his mother had been attacked and thrown out of her home. As a teen, she'd been homeless and pregnant. Abandoned.

Yes, Menyara had taken her in, but now that he knew the truth . . .

Nick wanted blood.

He glared at Menyara. "How could you do that to my mother? You cost her everything!"

"It wasn't supposed to happen the way it did, Nicholas. We had her hidden, in safety, we thought. She was given a good home, with a kind, loving family, who cared deeply for her. But her light burns so bright that it can't be disguised or denied. Somehow, she summoned Adarian before we were ready for it. He found her years before she was meant to find him." She reached out to brush the hair back from his face. "I am so sorry for the pain we caused you and Cherise. We never meant for that to happen. You have to believe me."

Nick's gaze fell to his mother's unconscious body. She looked so young. And she was. Most women her age were just starting their families, not saddled with a teenager. "I'm not the one you should apologize to, Mennie. I'm not the one you hurt. You ruined her life."

Worse than that, Mennie let *him* ruin it. And that was what hurt most of all.

Menyara shook her head in denial. "She would be the first to disagree. You know that, Nicholas. That's what makes her so incredibly special. What gives us hope that you might be able to have a different outcome from the other Malachais before you. You are the only one since the firstborn who was raised by a mother who loves you. A Malachai who unites both the light and the dark. You do not have to strictly be a force of destruction. Because of your mother's love, you can choose to be a force for good, instead."

Honestly? Right now, he wasn't thinking good, happy thoughts. He was all about doing harm to everyone who'd had a hand in setting his mom up for this life.

But Menyara's words made him flinch as he remembered the sight of Ambrose earlier. His future self hadn't predicted a happy outcome by any means. He'd been on the brink of conversion. And his premonitions didn't give him a whole lot to look forward to, either.

From the way things were looking, he was basically screwed. And there was no way to avert his destiny.

Yeah, he was feeling pretty dang defeated.

Lied to. Kicked in the stones.

And extremely pissed off by all of this. "I don't even know you anymore, lady. Everything you've ever told me was a lie. And I do mean every single thing out of your mouth. Even your name. Now you expect me to believe this? To trust you? How can I trust you ever again?"

"I'm still your aunt Mennie."

Yeah, right. Was she?

Was she Menyara, the Voodoo priestess and Creole midwife who delivered him, or the Egyptian goddess Ma'at, who was related to Kody? Or the ancient primal goddess Cam, related to Caleb and Xev?

How could she just keep changing her identities and relationships like people discarded their socks? It completely boggled those last three brain cells that rattled around his head.

"No. You're a stranger to me. Someone who used my mother for her own gain, and seriously hurt her, all the while telling her she could trust you." Nick dodged her hand as she reached to touch him. He wasn't in the mood for it. Too much was happening, too fast.

Honestly, he didn't know whom to trust, at this point.

Except himself. While he knew Ambrose wasn't exactly sane, he knew he'd never lie to himself. Especially not about his mother and her well-being.

That was the only thing he could bank on for certain. Ambrose only wanted to save his mother.

Everyone else, even Kody, could be lying to him, for all he really knew. He didn't want to be that jaded, but he had to face the fact that it could be true. Livia had been one hundred percent right.

No one could be trusted.

He didn't know what was what anymore. Everything and everyone around him seemed like a lie. His head spun from it all. Truthfully? He just wanted to feel grounded again. To have some kind of anchor he could count on that wouldn't leave him feeling lost and adrift.

"Am I even Cajun?"

Menyara laughed. "Yes, Nicholas. That you are. Your real grandmother was a true blue zydeco-playing backwoods Cajun that would have made you proud."

Well, at least he still had that. Thank goodness. He wasn't sure he could have handled learning he was something weird like the grandson of millionaire mining tycoon.

Thunder clapped and the lights blinked as they tried to come on.

Sadly, the darkness returned and reminded him what he needed to do. "I have to find the Eye of Ananke to straighten this mess out. Has anyone heard of it?"

Four pairs of eyes glanced around aimlessly and refused to meet his gaze, letting him know that as usual he, alone, was the idiot in the room. "What?"

"Where did you hear that term?" Mennie asked.

Nick started not to answer her. He really didn't owe her any answers given how many lies she'd told him over the years. But at this point . . .

Why bother? He was worn out by the lies and tired of playing games. "Ambrose told me to find it."

Mennie scowled. "Ambrose?"

"Yeah. Future me. Apparently, centuries from now, after I get pimp-slapped with a Dark-Hunter bow on my face—really wish Artemis had chosen a better location on my body to mark me with that—and I'm on the brink of morphing into the full soulless Malachai who's bent on binge-punishing humanity, I eat a demon that has time-traveling abilities. Sad to say, they don't last long, and I just used the last of it to come here and tell me to get the Eye, and use it to reset whatever it is we screwed up." He glanced to Kody. "So what is this thing and where is it?"

Giddy with excitement, Simi raised her hand. "Ooo, ooo, ooo, the Simi finally knows an answer! It in that scary, scary room, in that scary temple in the lowest level of Hades's domain. Least it used to be and I doubts anybody's moved it 'cause that ugly, snarly dogs thing with all them heads gets really nasty whenever someone goes down there. And them dragons and snake-headed people not real happy 'bout it neither."

Kody nodded. "Uh, yeah, that would be correct. Cerberus and the gorgons can be a little territorial whenever someone ventures into Tartarus to disturb it."

It was her turn to be gaped at.

"What?" She blinked innocently. "I played hide-and-seek there as a kid. Uncle Hades holds great Halloween parties. But . . . I can't exactly go waltzing in there right now as no one knows who I am, since I won't be born for another few hundred years."

Menyara sighed. "I'm definitely not welcomed

there. During my tenure as the Egyptian goddess Ma'at, my pantheon was at war with the Olympians. They would know the instant I stepped foot in their realm, and attack me full-on."

Xev crossed his arms over his chest. "The one thing my childhood taught me was how to hide my powers and pass through realms where I wasn't wanted. It was how I was able to visit my wife undetected beneath the noses of the Sephirii, who were well trained to hunt and kill my kind."

He locked gazes with Kody. "While I know what it is, I don't know what it looks like. If someone can tell me what I'm looking for and where it's located, I can retrieve it."

Menyara scoffed at his offer. "It's not that simple. Only a god of fate can touch it without being destroyed by it."

Kody chewed her lip. "I share your bloodline through my mother. Can I touch it?"

"Given your father's blood, I don't know. Especially since he once shared a womb with Acheron. You're also no longer in your true body. . . . I have no idea what would happen to you should you touch it. It's not worth the chance of finding out."

Nick let out a nervous laugh. "Personally, I vote Girlfriend stays here with Simi to watch over my mother in the event whatever nabbed her before comes back for Round Two."

Xev shook his head. "Either Girlfriend or Charonte will be needed to lead us both in to retrieve it, since I know nothing of Hades." He arched a brow at Menyara. "What is this Hades, anyway?"

"The Olympians were children of the Titans, who became Greek gods after you were cursed and banished."

Kody passed an irritated smirk to Nick. "Why can't Simi and I both go?"

Nick gestured at the non-working lights. "Hello? Unnatural storm? We have Yrre on the loose. Memitims at the windows. *Zeitjägers* in the corners. Now Tiamat. A spewing Caleb. Unconscious Mom. Zavid's AWOL, and I don't know what to think about Livia. Anyone else want to add anything to my growing super-sized ulcer?"

A sudden knock on the door made Nick jump with an undignifying sound he really wished Kody hadn't heard. For that matter, he hated that anyone had witnessed it. Disgusted with himself, he glared up at the ceiling. "Hello, up there? That was *not* meant as a personal challenge."

Cringing, he went to open the door, forgetting about the peephole. A mistake he realized too late when he opened the door and learned that yeah, evil did, in fact, knock politely.

And a whole lot of it stood in his hallway, engulfed by flames, glaring straight at him.

CHAPTER 9

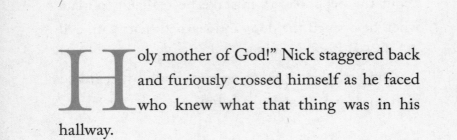

"Holy mother of God!" Nick staggered back
and furiously crossed himself as he faced
who knew what that thing was in his
hallway.

It wasn't so much that the male entity had a couple
of inches on him in height—which was impressive, as
few beings topped his six-foot-four stance—as it was
the muscled girth of him. And the aura of absolute
malevolent blood-thirst that said he was here to make
Nick-McNuggets.

Long, jet-black hair was pulled back into a ponytail from sharp, perfectly chiseled features that belonged to some ancient Asian warlord who should be

leading a conquering army of some kind. Bloodred eyes glared at Nick from beneath an irate glower that would make Kyrian proud.

Nick screamed and tried to shut the door.

Quicker than Nick could blink, he reached over his shoulder and unsheathed a curved, flaming sword. He swung it so fast, he would have taken Nick's head had Xev not caught the blade with his own sword and forced the demon back.

The demon's eyes widened with recognition. "I don't want to hurt you, Dar. Either get out of my way or I'm going through you." That was one serious accent on him. Unlike anything Nick had ever heard before. It was fluid and musical, and filled with murderous intent.

"Why are you here?"

He answered by becoming a shadow that swept through and around Xev to rematerialize behind him. He moved toward the couch where Nick's mom slept.

Xev became a multicolored wisp of smoke that wrapped around the newcomer's face and neck. The newcomer dissolved to re-form into the warrior so that he could fight Xev. They faced off to battle like the ancient gods they were. Nick put himself between Kody and his mother while Simi and Menyara formed a wall in front of him.

Nick had a bad feeling they weren't a lot of protection, but it was better than nothing.

Xev spun with his sword. The other god ducked and caught him a hard blow to his jaw. Unfazed, Xev knocked him to the side. Instead of moving, he dissolved to stab Xev, who vanished only to reappear behind him. It was a crazy, impressive fight as they fought as clouds of smoke, men and beasts that gave Nick a whole new appreciation for the kind of warfare they must have used in battle during the Primus Bellum.

The kind of tactics he'd one day use as the Malachai against Kody and her army.

"Who is that?" Nick asked Mennie.

"Dagon." Menyara sighed wearily.

He mouthed the name to Kody, who shrugged to let him know she had no idea, either. "Could you expand a few details?" he tried again.

"Son of Noir and Hekate."

Kody scowled. "*My* Hekate?"

"Yes."

Nick wasn't sure why that name rang his bell, but something about Dagon's mother was familiar to him. "Why do I know her name?"

Instead of Menyara, it was Kody who answered while Simi cheered Xev on and even offered him her bottle of barbecue sauce should he need it. "Tabitha Devereaux and her sisters talk about her, and Kyrian has a couple of her statues in his house. Hekate's a good friend of my cousin Katra, and Persephone. She's the Greek goddess of necromancy, magic, spirits, and the night."

Ah . . . now he remembered seeing those statues littered around Kyrian's mansion. She was one of the goddesses Kyrian would occasionally swear upon whenever Nick really ticked him off about something.

But one thing struck him as odd about a Greek goddess. . . . "And she hooked up with the lord of all darkness whose name I can't say without empowering him and sending out a homing signal for him to come kill me? The same malevolent creature who happens to be your"—he glared at Menyara—"brother?"

Menyara nodded. "Believe it or not, he can be quite charming when he's not psychotic. And Hekate has always had a thing for bad boys."

Yeah, but getting it on with the original source of all evil and then spawning with him? That took it to a whole new I-need-some-serious-therapy level. He really didn't want to know about her daddy issues.

Nick rubbed at his throbbing temples as he watched Xev and Dagon crash into his mother's prized curio and shatter it. Ugh, he was in so much trouble for this. He was going to be grounded for all eternity.

And given the fact he could conceivably live that long, the threat actually had merit.

"How do we break this up before they destroy my mom's entire house and I get grounded until I'm decrepit?"

Menyara sighed. "Not sure."

Mazel tov! His ulcer just had a baby. And it was quickly mutating to the size of nuclear Godzilla. "Do they even know why they're fighting?"

"I don't think it matters."

Simi let out an ear-splitting whistle. Xev and Dagon paused to frown at her. "Hello? Ancient annoying ones? You are stressing out the Simi's good quality friend and making Akri-Nick very sad, and that makes the Simi very sad. Could you please find an old field to fight in where you don't break his mama's things and get him grounded? He don't like when that happens. And it make Akra-Kody sad, too, 'cause then she has to sneak in to see him and risk getting into trouble if his mama be hearing them in his room, and they shouldn't be doing that, and they both know it. Bad, bad, bad."

His breathing ragged, Dagon wiped at the blood on his lips as he finally noticed their small group. He scowled in disbelief. "Is that a Charonte?" he asked Xev.

"It is."

"Alone?"

"Not exactly."

He arched a brow at that before he looked to Menyara. "Apollymi's free?"

She shook her head. "She's still in captivity, but her son remains alive and free, and protects Simi as his child."

His gaze went to Kody before his jaw dropped. "Bethany?" She was the Atlantean goddess of wrath.

"No. I'm her daughter."

Appearing even more confused, Dagon sheathed his sword and straightened his clothes. His expression said he was struggling to make sense of everything, and not quite able to do so.

Xev sheathed his sword and wiped at the blood on his own face. "How long have *you* been held, brother?"

Dagon rubbed at his scarred wrist. "Since the reign of Etana."

Menyara sucked her breath in sharply.

By her reaction, Nick knew it had to be a long time ago, but unfortunately, history wasn't one of his better subjects. Though, to be honest, he was quickly learning. "When was that?"

Menyara sighed heavily. "Almost five thousand years ago."

Wow! Nick wheezed at the realization while Dagon

winced. "Dude! What'd you do? That takes being grounded to a whole new level! Jeez, I'm so glad my mama can't hear that one. She might get ideas I don't need her to."

Simi's eyes widened. She made a sharp squeak as if she finally put two and two together. "That was *you* what done that with Zeus and them Arcadians and gots into all that trouble? Ooo, I remember that. That was so bad for you, but so nice for you to do! You the Simi's hero."

Nick arched his brow. "You, what? What'd he do?"

It was Menyara who answered. "He's the one who taught the ancient king Lycaon how to save his cursed sons and use sorcery to merge their blood with that of animals and create the race of Were-Hunters."

Shocked to the core of his being, Nick stared at Dagon. He'd always wondered how Lycaon had learned to do something that powerful.

Back during the human lifetime of Acheron, the Greek god Apollo had become enraged at the race of beings he'd created and named after himself—the Apollites—for their queen ordering the death of his mistress and child. To retaliate for it, Apollo had cursed everyone born of the Apollite race to die horribly at age twenty-seven, the same age his mistress had been when they slaughtered her.

The Atlantean goddess Apollymi had stepped in and showed a handful of Apollites how to survive the curse by taking human souls into their bodies and using them to artificially elongate their lives. Once those so-called Daimons had begun preying on humanity, and to protect mankind, Apollo's twin sister Artemis had created the Dark-Hunters to hunt them down and kill them before the human soul inside them died, and free it so that it could go on to its eternal resting place.

For thousands of years, that had been the order of things. A small number of rogue Apollites became Daimons and were put down for their murderous needs by Dark-Hunters like Kyrian and Acheron.

Until an innocent Arcadian king, Lycaon, had unknowingly taken an Apollite bride. She'd given him two sons before she died tragically on her twenty-seventh birthday, per Apollo's curse.

Grief-stricken, the king had turned to his gods for

help and they had refused him. So the legend said he'd begun using the darkest of magic to merge the life force of the strongest animals with that of the Apollites until he found the two best matches for his sons.

With each experiment that started with two creatures, an Apollite and an animal, it produced an Apollite who could shift into an animal—a so-called Arcadian. And an animal who could take the form of an Apollite—a Katagari. Two separate humanlike races who were no longer condemned to die on their twenty-seventh birthday. Instead, they were imbued with extreme psychic gifts and a much slower rate of aging. One that allowed them to live for hundreds of years.

For his hybris in thwarting Apollo's will, Lycaon was cursed by the Greek gods. They demanded that he kill the creatures he'd created, including his own sons. When he refused, the Were-Hunters he'd made out of desperation to save his children were condemned to know no peace. For the rest of time, the Katagaria and Arcadians were doomed to be at war and to fight until no more of their kind were left.

It was a war that still continued, and it was why Stone and Alex, as well as other Were-Hunters in Nick's school, were constantly going at each other.

Nick had always wondered how Lycaon had learned that dark magic to create a whole new species. Now he knew. The answer for it stood in his living room.

Dagon.

Even as a god himself, Dagon definitely had a set to defy the others of his kind. Not many cells in the head, but a huge set in the trousers. "Are you serious? You gave that knowledge and ability to Lycaon?"

Dagon gave a subtle nod. "And like Prometheus, I was punished for it."

Xev frowned. "Why would you help an Arcadian king?"

"Why ever do you think, cousin? He implored my Shala. She cried. I acted."

Menyara turned toward Nick. "Dagon was the ancient Akkadian god of seasons, magic, and time."

Xev arched a shocked brow at her list. "That's not the ruthless god I remember. In my day, he, alongside

Cam, judged the dead and was one of his father's best generals during the Primus Bellum. He was a war god then who served the Malachai army well, and gleefully slaughtered everyone who came near him. What changed you?"

Menyara let out an ironic laugh. "As you told Nick earlier, Dagon went to see his mother one afternoon, and met the goddess of compassion, Shala. She changed everything about him. Gave him a heart and a soul."

Dagon's features turned to stone. "And it is for Shala that I've come. Because of me, Noir still holds her and I have to awaken Azura in this realm. Now stand aside." He started for the couch.

They all blocked his way.

"Yeah, buddy, that ain't gonna happen." Nick stepped forward. "You need to leave now. Either out the door or through a window. Your choice."

Fire rolled over Dagon's shoulders. "Out of my way, boy. You have no idea who you're dealing with."

Nick unfurled his wings and for the first time ever, he let his true Malachai fly. He knew it was all hanging out by the way Menyara and Kody gasped. "The last fool who called me boy ended up as a stain on the bottom of my shoe."

Licking his fangs, he narrowed his eyes on the ancient god. "You want to dance, name the tune. Just remember, I ain't Xev and I hold no love, kinship, nor friendship toward you."

Dagon came at him with the same massive attack he'd used on Xev.

Instead of trying to fight him, Nick grabbed his arm and jerked him off balance. He spun the god around, buried his hand in his ponytail, and yanked his head back, exposing his neck. Before he could stop himself, his instincts kicked in and he buried his fangs in the god's jugular.

Dagon tried to vanish. Somehow Nick kept him from it. He had no idea how. Something inside him just knew instinctively how to keep him in his form and under restraint. It was like a baby breathing or suckling its mother's milk.

More than that, Nick's senses reeled as he drank the power and tapped the Source that had birthed them both. Though he'd never been drunk, he had a good idea that this was what it must feel like. His senses sharpened so that he could hear everything in the aether. Every heartbeat for miles around.

He couldn't really explain it. It was like being tapped into some kind of cosmic database for every living thing in the universe.

And he knew he was about to kill Dagon. Strangely, that wasn't what frightened him. What terrified him to the core of his being was the part of him that craved it. The ease with which he could end Dagon and not care at all.

In fact, he would relish it.

Startled by that realization, he let go and staggered back.

Kody reached out for him. "Nick?"

His blood rushed through his veins with the familiar lust he always felt in her presence. But this time, it wasn't carnal lust.

It was for her blood.

Her life. He wanted to end her. Desperately.

Simi stepped toward him.

He hissed and slashed with his claws, aiming for her throat, wanting to rip it out, too.

Menyara barely caught Simi in time and saved her from the attack.

Kody couldn't breathe as she saw the unfeeling demon inside Nick's eyes. The searing hatred that bore no recognition of them. This wasn't the boy she knew and loved. The loyal friend who would cut his own throat before he betrayed those closest to him.

This was the beast who'd callously murdered her and her entire family.

The Malachai who'd coldly snapped Caleb's neck and stepped over his body without a second thought.

Anguish choked her as she remembered that fateful day and she saw her brother's death in her mind. As she felt helpless to save Ari's life.

And her own.

This was the beast they were all trying so hard to prevent Nick from becoming.

"Menyara?"

But Menyara was as horrified as she and Simi. Unlike her, this was the first time Menyara had seen

instinct

Nick in this form. The first time Menyara faced the full Ambrose Malachai. And he was a fierce, frightening beast.

Xev grabbed Kody in a firm hold. "Kiss him."

She widened her eyes. "Are you out of your mind?" Nick was more likely to kill her than welcome her while in this state.

"Trust me."

"Are you out of your mind?" she repeated.

"Do it!"

Before she could protest again, he shoved her against Nick. Only this wasn't Nick. This was the monster Malachai. Huge and muscled, he glared down at her with a hatred that terrified her. There was no recognition in those glowing red eyes. No humanity or soul.

They were searing.

He growled at her and she waited for him to rip out her throat, and laugh while he did it.

Every part of Kody wanted to run, screaming, for cover. But her mother had been the great Bathymaas of antiquity, the original goddess of justice—Bethany of Atlantis and Egypt—a goddess of unbelievable power and courage. Her father had been Styxx Anaxkolasi of the House of Aricles, prince of Didymos. One of the greatest ancient generals to ever lead an army, and one of the strongest of the Chthonians to ever live. She would not dishonor them or herself by backing down from any threat.

Not even this one.

With every molecule of courage she could muster, she faced the demon before her and held her ground. Hoping and praying Xev wasn't setting her up to die, she laid her hand on Nick's mottled cheek and searched those foreign eyes for a sign of something familiar.

All she saw was hatred and despair.

"Nick?" she whispered, aching to reach him before he was lost to them forever. "Can you hear me?"

Are you still in there somewhere?

Please be in there, somewhere. . . .

He cocked his head to study her and narrowed his flame-filled eyes.

With her other hand, she reached up to trace his brow as she did whenever they were alone in his condo.

"I need my sweet Cajun to come back to me. Who else is going to translate all the things in this city I don't understand like '*fais do-do*,' 'fixin' to,' 'makin' groceries,' and 'neutral ground,' and tell me the difference between *bebette* and *bebelle*?"

"*Bebelle, cher.*" Though he still remained in full Malachai form, she heard the slight softening of his demonic voice in the whispered endearment he only used for her.

You better be right about this, Xev.

Completely petrified, she buried her hand in his sleek black hair and slowly lowered his lips to hers. At first, he growled angrily, and started to pull away, but the moment her tongue swept against his, he changed. His arms hesitantly wrapped around her body to hold her in a gentle embrace as his wings came down. Those wings cocooned them in a feathery caress before they finally vanished with the lightest stirring of air.

He brought his hands up to cup her head in a gentle, familiar hold. His hair changed from the sleek demon texture to the soft waves she was used to burying her hands in.

When Kody opened her eyes, she no longer stared into those red, searing orbs, but the beautiful blue eyes that held a part of her no one else ever had. She had no idea why Nick thought Zavid, Xev, and Caleb were more handsome than he was. They had nothing on her sharp-witted, smart-aleck Cajun.

Well, *maybe* a better wardrobe.

But even in his wrinkled mass of oversized, tacky, hideous Hawaiian shirts, Nicholas Gautier turned heads and left her breathless.

Smiling up at him, she ran her fingertip over his bottom lip. *"Ca c'est bon, n'est pas?"*

That familiar charming grin that never failed to turn her to mush and get him out of any amount of trouble where she and his mother were concerned curved his lips. *"Oui. Toujours, cher."*

How could any male be so dang charismatic? Yes, he had the Malachai's glamour that charmed people, but his went deeper than that. There was something much more compelling about Nick. Something that made her feel warm and safe whenever he was near. Honestly, she never wanted to leave his company.

Never wanted to be any place except right here, in his embrace.

Crossing his arms over his chest, Xev gave her a smug smirk. "Our weaknesses. Forever."

Kody paused at that thought and let it roll around in her mind.

Had they changed the future already? Could it be possible? If she *could* call Nick back from his full Malachai form, could she prevent him from ending the world?

Was *this* the answer they sought?

Dagon laughed bitterly as he pushed himself up from the floor. Pale and weak from what Nick had done to him, he struggled to stand. "You're a naive child, aren't you?"

"What?" she asked.

"I can hear the thoughts churning in your mind. They're written all over your face. It doesn't matter how much sway you hold over him. In fact, the more of him you hold, the weaker he becomes."

"How so?"

Xev met Dagon's gaze before he answered Kody's

question. "Because whatever weakness you have becomes Nick's weakness. Don't you understand? What happened to me happened not because *I* was vulnerable. It happened because my wife and Caleb's wife were threatened and couldn't protect themselves. The actions we took were to keep them safe from our enemies. That was our mistake and our damnation. Even Dagon was punished and condemned over his wife's compassion for her brother, Lycaon. Not his own."

Nodding, Dagon wiped at his neck. His gaze returned to Cherise. "I have to have the woman. She is a blood tie to the Source. Azura needs her body to enter this world. If I help her cross over, she will free Shala."

When he took a step forward, Menyara blocked him. "Azura can't do that."

"Cam—"

"Dagon . . . Shala's dead. You know she is. Noir killed her long ago. Use your powers and ask your mother. Look into your heart and tap the Source yourself. You know I speak the truth, honey."

Shaking his head in denial, he staggered back. "No. She lives. She has to. I gave up my freedom . . . my life for hers. That was the bargain I made with them."

"They lied to you and I'm sorry. A part of her essence still exists in Eleos, but the Shala you knew . . . they destroyed her centuries ago."

Dagon stood frozen, as if the words were so much more than he could bear to hear.

Tears welled in Kody's eyes as she saw the raw pain in his. She felt terrible for the ancient god.

A tic started in his jaw as a single tear slid down his cheek. "I should have known better than to trust my father when he swore to me that he'd never harm her. I should have known he'd never keep his word to me." His lips trembled as he met Menyara's gaze. "Did she suffer?"

"No."

But they all knew she was lying, too.

Placing his hand on Dagon's shoulder, Xev ground his teeth. "I'm so sorry."

Fire rolled over his shoulders, forcing Xev to jerk his hand back with a grimace. Dagon pulled a small, ornate bottle from his sleeve. "They wanted me to give this to the woman so that Azura could be reborn into her body."

Menyara shook her head. "Don't do what you're thinking, Dagon."

An evil smile spread across his handsome face. "Why not? A little divine retribution might go a long way in making all of us feel better."

"Do I want to know what you're thinking?" Xev asked.

"Not if you wish to remain in one piece. I'm sure your mother would rip you to shreds should you participate in my plans to have Azura reborn as a pig."

Suddenly, there was a deep, dark crash of thunder followed by lightning so bright, it was blinding. It shook the entire building.

Nick grabbed the back of the couch to steady himself. "What the hell-monkey visits us now?"

His features pale, Xev went to the window and opened the curtains so that Nick could see that it wasn't just the Memitim on the street. The sky was now filled with more birds than he'd ever seen in his life.

At least to human eyes they appeared as birds. With his perspicacity, Nick saw them for what they really were.

Soldiers in an army that was here to kill Nick and everyone who stood with him.

Nick sighed heavily. "I *really* shouldn't have said hell-monkey."

CHAPTER 10

Xev turned on Dagon. "Claim a side to die for."

Dagon frowned as his gaze went from Simi to Kody to Menyara and Nick. "Fine, but I'm not sure what side *this* is. Are you?"

"Meaning?"

He scowled at Nick's hand on Kody's. "Since when does the Malachai fight beside Cam and the daughter of Bathymaas?"

Nick flashed him a devilish grin. "I'm not your average Malachai."

"So it's true, then. There is a Malachai born of the light?"

Xev hesitated about confirming it in so many words. "He fights against Noir and Azura."

"And the ušumgallu?" Dagon asked. Not that Nick blamed him for being suspicious. Before picking a side in a war this deadly and scary, it paid to ask a few questions and do some homework. Once a flag was chosen, it was hard to surrender it. "Where do they and their allies stand in this?"

"Mostly undeclared. Malphas is temporarily down, but fights with us, unequivocally. Livia is with us. Bane undecided. We know nothing of Grim or Laguerre. We assume Yrre is against us, but we don't know for certain."

Nick grimaced as he realized his allies were even fewer than he'd thought.

Ouch.

Dagon's gaze went to the window, where it narrowed sharply. "I'd say they've declared enmity. Those carrions are seeking Malachai blood. Once they have it, you'll have no choice. You either ride with Death and War. Or die." He scowled at Nick. "Why didn't you drain your šarras while you could?"

In retrospect?

Stupidity.

But that wasn't what he said out loud. He answered with the truth. "I didn't think I had to. Caleb said all I had to do was confront them, show them who's boss, and seal the gate. We did that. Yrre was never released. Only Livia and Xev, and they relented to me. At least that's what I was told."

"Someone lied to you. Yrre made it through to this side, and is roaming free."

Nick searched his memory as he tried to remember who'd told him that Yrre had stayed sealed in. For his life, he couldn't recall who'd said that.

Crap. Where had that come from? He knew he hadn't imagined it. Someone had told him that. Had they set him up intentionally? Could they have meant to betray him or was it a misunderstanding or mistake?

And if it was intentional . . .

I'm so screwed.

No, worse than that. Someone would have intentionally betrayed him. Set him up for this so that they'd all get their butts handed to them in this massacre.

He passed a look between Kody, Xev, and Dagon. "So what do we do?"

Dagon hesitated before he answered. "Where are the Arelim or Sephiroth?"

Snorting with bitter amusement, Xev looked at Nick with a smirk that said he'd let him explain. Oh goody!

Nick was less than amused as he ran with the cue. "The last Sephiroth is imprisoned. I have no idea where. From what I've been told, I don't want to know where, either, as it's highly unpleasant. The Arelim are in the middle of a horrific civil war, and both sides hate my guts with a passion that burns brighter than a binary star system. Needless to say, we're a little low on allies. I do have a few Dark-Hunters and two lunatics I can count on. Along with one awesome Charonte."

Simi grinned.

Menyara sighed heavily. "He's right. Rezar is missing. Verlyn captured. Our side has been losing ground for a long time now, which is another reason why we had to secure the Malachai and limit his powers any way we could. But that being said, I can summon Acheron and Savitar, as well as Thorn."

Dagon cocked his head. "Thorn?"

"Leucious of the Brakadians," Menyara explained. "He and his Hellchasers are still firmly against Noir and Azura. Though their numbers aren't many, they're as strong as ever, and they fight them every chance they get."

Xev inclined his head to Menyara. "Summon them all and do it fast. We need every sword."

No sooner had he spoken than a strange light permeated the room, washing it with a weird glow that came from outside.

Dread filled every pore of Nick's body. "What is that?"

"Takiramon," Dagon and Xev said in unison.

"And that would be what brand of Pokémon, Ash Ketchum? Should I fetch Pikachu's ball and have at it? I choose *you*, Dagon!"

Rolling her eyes at Nick's sarcasm that went over Xev's and Dagon's heads, Kody let go of Nick's hand

and summoned her Arelim battle armor and swords. "It's the veil of mortal sleep."

"The who . . . what?"

Kody checked her weapons. "Veil of mortal sleep. There aren't many creatures strong enough to conjure it. It casts that red glow over the earth and puts the humans into a trance so that they are unaware of us. . . . Like your mother, they sleep, completely safe, and totally ignorant of what's happening around them." Kody jerked her chin toward the window. "See for yourself."

Nick went to look, and sure enough. Everyone outside, who'd been walking around just a few minutes ago, was lying sprawled out on the sidewalks like corpses in open graves. It was creepy and chilling—not something anyone wanted to see outside of a zombie movie.

His blood ran cold at the unnatural sight that left him terrified for the world and everyone in it. Worse, it made him feel powerless against who or whatever had sent *that*. How could they even begin to fight against something so powerful? Were they nuts?

"Are they okay?" he asked Xev.

"For the moment."

"Meaning?"

Kody sighed nervously. "They're easy pickings. If we don't do something, they won't be okay for long. Anything or anyone could attack them. And if they stay that way until morning, they're all dead. There won't be any way to bring them back, then. Including your mom."

Simi spread her wings and broke out her barbecue sauce. "The Simi ready to battle and chow down. Show me them demons! It's snack time!"

Kody turned to Nick as he felt his eyes starting to change to demon red. "You need to stay mortal. Keep your Malachai powers leashed."

"Why?"

"Because you can't control them. Every time you break them out, we lose a part of you. Can't you feel it?"

At the moment, what he felt was sick to his stomach that all of this was happening to innocent people because of him and what they'd failed to do.

Protect them.

"She's right, Nick." Xev stepped closer to him. "I saw it, too. We barely got you back earlier. Another minute, and I'm not sure we would have."

Dagon brushed at the bloody wound on his neck. "Since I was the one bitten and I'm still weak from it, I concur. You don't need to invoke powers you can't control. It's just a real bad idea."

Menyara strengthened the spells for the condo. "We're still hidden here. They can't find us. Stay with Cherise while I get our reinforcements." She vanished instantly.

"I don't like staying here and waiting," Nick shouted at Menyara, but she was already gone and didn't hear a word of it.

Irritated, he watched as the birds began to land on the ground and transform into demonic warriors who searched the bodies as if looking for someone. And he had a bad idea that person was either him or Caleb. "We need to get to Caleb's and protect him."

Dagon snorted. "You use that kind of power and they will sense it instantly, follow you, and attack."

"He's right," Xev concurred. "They'd be all over us."

"So what do we do? The Hokey-Pokey? Turn ourselves around? Feed them my best friend and say *bon appetit*? 'Cause no offense, I'm not really okay with that. Caleb's been there for me since the very beginning. He's bled for me when no one else has, and has never failed to save my butt. So you can stand here, watching *Demon Kingdom* out there, which is a *fascinating* show, all you want to, but I'm going to stand and fight for my friend."

Dagon's frown deepened. "Is he always like this?"

Xev nodded. "I told you. He's not like the others of his ilk."

"No . . . definitely not. All the Malachais I've known would have hand-fed Malphas to their enemies to buy themselves time to get soldiers." His tone said Dagon wasn't so sure that was a good thing, though.

Nick's grin widened. "Relax. It's just all the paint chips I ate as a kid. No real lasting damage. Ignore the extra finger and toe. They actually come in handy and toey at times."

And that, too, appeared lost on the ancient god

who had no measurable sense of humor. How very sad for him.

Groaning as if his bad jokes caused her physical pain, Kody shook her head.

Simi wrapped her arm around Nick's shoulder. "So, it demon chow time? The Simi getting hungry while the buffet is down there and getting bigger in number. I vote the Simi go cull the herd while we wait." She flashed an eager grin.

Nick returned his attention to the army that was marching nearer, searching for them. As he watched, a strange thought went through him.

Maybe, just maybe, there was some hope left.

He glanced over to the two ancient former gods. "I'm Patton, right?"

They exchanged a puzzled frown.

"Patton?" Xev asked.

Yeah, that reference was probably lost on them. "General of the great demon horde out there? I guess in your days, a like comparison would have been Styxx of Didymos, since you both predate Alexander the Great."

Nick scowled as he realized what he'd just said. "Wait. How do I know that? I know nothing about history. Holy crap, I was actually listening when Ash and Kyrian talk? Don't nobody ever tell them that. They might get more egotistical and we'd have to find a bigger house for it." He jerked his chin toward the demons. "Anyway, they might answer to another commander for now, but ultimately that commander is my bitch, right?"

Dagon had an expression that said Nick had lost him around the bend.

Luckily, Xev was keeping pace. "Yes. Your point?"

"What would I need to do to go out there and claim them as my guys?"

Kody snorted. "A miracle."

"Not helping," Nick said drily.

Xev took a deep breath before he slid a speculative glance toward Simi. "A miracle," he repeated and concurred.

Nick rolled his eyes.

Xev cracked an irritating grin. "You can always go out there with your charming personality and try to win them over." He nudged Nick toward the door. "Go on. I dare you."

Nick headed for the door. "I will. I mean, think about it. Everyone attacks them, right? They're used to fighting. If I go out there to talk to them, it'll throw them off guard. It worked earlier when I talked to the Memitims. No one attacked me. They actually seemed kind of reasonable. So if I go out there and assert myself, tell them that I'm their supreme poobah, they'll fall in line, right?"

"To kill you?" Xev asked. "Most likely. To listen and obey? Wouldn't stake *my* life on it. But far be it from me to interfere with your stupidity, in any way."

Nick shrugged his hold off. "Ha, ha. Real funny." He swept his gaze over them. "Anyone got something better?"

"Molotov cocktails?" Simi volunteered. "That way, they be cooking while they fleeing."

Choking on Simi's solution, Kody bit her lip in a most adorable way. "I might have an idea. But I'm not sure you're going to like it."

"Okay. Let's hear it."

Before Kody could tell Nick her plan, everything in the room froze. Even time itself.

Only Nick seemed unaffected by whatever was causing it. Was this the Takiramon? Could it also affect preters? He had no other explanation.

At least nothing that made any sense.

Even Simi was frozen in place and that *never* happened. Nothing like this ever affected her. Nick waved his hand before her face, half expecting her to bite at his fingers and laugh at him for being so gullible.

She didn't.

What is this?

He poked gently at Simi. She didn't move or flinch at all. His heart pounding, he heard the shrieking sound of a horse from outside his window. Literally, right outside his window.

With a fierce scowl, he went to investigate. As soon as he parted the curtains, he jumped back with a startled piercing shout that would have rivaled scream-queen Marilyn Burns confronting Leatherface. Not the manliest sound he'd ever made. Thank goodness none of the others could bear witness to it.

Outside the window, floating in midair, was the king of the plague doctors. Only this guy looked like he'd not only gotten the plague, he'd picked up scabies, rabies, and a few other flesh-rotting diseases along the way.

A bony finger emerged from bloody robes to point at Nick and motion him outside.

Nick shook his head. "Sorry. I'm grounded. My mom won't let me come out and play until all my homework and chores are done. Should be at least a decade or so . . . maybe a couple of centuries."

It held up a large hourglass that only had a few grains of sand. "When this empties, if you're not out here, Malachai, everyone you love will die."

Nick scoffed until he realized there was a *zeitjäger* standing over everyone in the room, with a bloody sickle angled for their throats.

Everyone.

Including his unconscious mother.

How was that possible?

Stunned, he looked back at the king of all death and realized the sands in the glass were almost gone.

CHAPTER 11

T here are some journeys we must take alone. Nick
paused as he heard his mother's voice in his
head with something she often said to him.
Birth. Death. Flossing. Toenail clipping. Bathroom breaks.

Garbage duty . . .

And apparently, facing whatever the heck that
thing was outside his condo that appeared to be in
charge of the *zeitjägers*.

All of those had to be done alone. Though to be
honest, he had a childish urge to run through the birds,
screaming like a hyperactive kid at the beach on a

massive sugar high. A part of him wondered if they'd take flight and scatter like other fowl creatures.

Most likely not.

His luck? They'd gut him where he stood and peck out his eyes. They didn't seem like the skittish type. More like the ones Zeus used to torture poor Prometheus for daring to give fire to mankind.

All right. Strap up, boy. Square those shoulders. Hold that head high. He was the Malachai. It was time to be the baddest beast in the land and show them who was boss.

But honestly? He wanted to tuck and run screaming in the opposite direction until there was nothing left of him except a vanishing vapor trail. The only thing that kept him from it was the number of people who were relying on him to be rock-steady. His mom. Kody. Caleb. Simi. Xev.

He refused to disappoint them.

They needed him to see this through. To be the man he pretended to be—the one he arrogantly professed to be whenever he was challenged. Not the boy he still felt like most days.

He wanted them to treat him like an adult. This was where adulthood began. And that was what being an adult meant. Handling crap you didn't want to deal with. Standing strong when you wanted to cave. He'd seen his mom do it enough to know the truth. How many times had she put on a brave face while hiding tears and dressing for a job that demeaned her and sucked out a part of her soul?

And how many times had he overheard her quiet morning pep talks she gave herself as she readied herself to face the coming horrors of a day?

Yet to feed him and keep a lousy roach-infested roof over their heads, she'd done it, day after day, while never once complaining about it.

You did what you had to.

Now it was his turn to strap on his big boy pants and save her and the others. *I can do this.*

Nick inhaled a deep breath to steady his nerves and released it as he flashed himself outside to face the demon lord, and see what the beast wanted with him.

One who was a heck of a lot larger up close than

he'd appeared through the window. What kind of steroids did he take? Dang!

Seriously subdued, Nick paused on the street with a grimace as he glanced around at the demons, who were also bigger up close and personal. Did they just multiply in number, too? He could have sworn there weren't this many a second ago.

Maybe that was just his nerves learning "new" math. Yeah. Could be.

As soon as they saw him, they moved into attack formation. Okay, that was even scarier than he'd anticipated.

Hold it together, Gautier. You've got this.

I don't got shite . . . are you blind?

Yeah, so much for his mom's self-help pep talks. They didn't work for squat. His gut was still tight enough to form a new diamond mine.

"Malachai!" His title went through their ranks like a hated whisper.

For one tiny, infinitesimal moment Nick thought when they did that, that would settle it. That they might run for cover like frightened rabbits.

Until he realized how right Xev had been. Their fear was more a rallying call than anything else. It made them even more unstable and hostile. More likely to attack him than to bolt.

Beautiful. Just beautiful. Scared, feral attack demons. Just what he'd asked for.

Never.

Tall and deadly, the cloaked demon lord approached him with a quirky smile twisting his lips. Scars covered his weathered face. Dressed black on black, he wore a hood over his head. Peculiar tarnished silver vambraces covered both of his forearms. Each one was embellished with an elaborate snake-and-egg design that seemed oddly familiar, though Nick had no idea why. Tendrils of dark hair framed his angular face as he studied Nick with an unamused stare.

"You're braver than I thought." More sand appeared in the hourglass he held. "Good. You bought yourself additional time with your courage. For that, I applaud you."

"Chronus, Chronus, Chronus," a strangely familiar feminine voice said in a staccato rhythm reminiscent of a clock's ticking. "You're being vague and the poor boy has no idea what you're talking about. And look at the poor thing. He's about to wet to his pants."

Tiamat appeared next to Nick's side with an adorable smile on her face. She brushed a lock of dark brown hair back from his forehead before she propped her arm on his shoulder and leaned against him. "Poor Malachai," she chided. "It's been a weird day for you, hasn't it?"

A chill went down his spine. "What's going on? What do you want with me?"

She laughed eerily before she pushed herself away from him and went to stand next to Chronus. "Think of it as a pop quiz. And you were doing unbelievably well."

"Were?" Nick felt his stomach starting to burn again.

Tiamat nodded. "We can't have the war starting *quite* yet. Not until *this* matter is settled."

Oh, he so didn't like the sound of any part of this. His ulcer was now the size of Texas and was currently having kittens *and* ducks. Probably a few lizards, too.

Pressing his hand against the gastric pain, Nick grimaced and wished he had a few gallons of Tums. "And what matter is that?"

"The head of the ušumgallu."

That took him by total surprise. What was she talking about? What head? *He* was the head, right?

"Excuse me?"

She stepped forward to pat his cheek in the most condescending way imaginable. The matrons at church would be so proud of how she did that. He was only surprised she didn't pinch his dimples while she was at it.

"A vote was called. It seems the majority of your generals feel you're unfit to lead them. And since there is another creature born of Adarian's blood, they are asking for us to judge which of you should be named his heir."

Nick forced himself not to gape or react in any way at something that had to be incredibly bad news for him. "I didn't think it worked that way."

She nodded. "The Malachai powers can be taken or assumed by another, especially a blood son, if one exists. It would be nothing for your older half brother to claim the birthright from you, should we deem him so worthy."

Oh goody! How about a good eye-gouging, too? Or groin-clamping? That sounded like even more fun!

But that brought him back to one stunning point that he still couldn't quite wrap his mind around.

"Wait . . . What? What older brother are we talking about? I didn't think the Malachai could have more than one son at a time who could live past the age of ten. Isn't that an impossibility?"

Chronos laughed. "Adarian was a crafty beast. Seems he found a way to bypass his curse, and hide his firstborn son from the gods. Something he confided to one of your šarras before he died. Like you, that son is being tested for his abilities, to see who is better suited for the Malachai role."

Tiamat patted his cheek. "This is where you should hope he fails and you pass."

Great. Talk about test anxiety. And in this case, Nick had a bad feeling failure wasn't an F.

It was a D . . . as in Death, and he didn't mean a party with Grim. Death as in dead in the grave, never to be seen or heard from again.

"And can I have some of the criteria on which I'm being judged?"

"No."

His jaw went slack at Tiamat's cold and unexpected answer. "No? Seriously? You're not going to give me a clue about how to pass this test or tell me anything about it?"

"No. That would take all the fun out of it. For us. But you've already completed a great deal of the test without even knowing, so breathe, child. We haven't killed you . . . yet. Relax."

Easy for her to say. No one was screwing with her life. "Yeah, but I like cheat codes."

A slow, insidious smile curved her lips. "Life isn't about cheat codes. It's about experience points."

Gah, they sounded like his mom. "So what's this next part of the test? Will you tell me that much?"

"You want to heal your mother and Malphas?" Chronus asked.

"More than anything."

"Then, knowing that more than half your generals are against you, you will have to choose two to trust. One to stay behind and protect your mother from your enemies should they attack her while you finish it. And one to stand at your back and fight with you and help you finish out your journey."

Chronus leaned in to whisper insidiously to Nick. "But be warned. Either one could betray you at any time, and use either you or your mother as a bargaining chip with your enemies to save themselves. That's the gamble you take."

Lovely. Lovely. Lovely.

"And if I choose not to play?"

Tiamat tsked at him. "Not an option."

Of course not. Nick ground his teeth as he cursed his luck and the Fates that had given him this life.

Tiamat wrinkled her nose at him. "So who will you choose to aid *you?*"

The first choice was an easy one to make. There was only one he'd put with his mother in his absence. "Xev to watch over my mom."

They both appeared shocked by his choice. Though why, he had no idea.

Until they spoke.

Chronus tilted his head curiously. "He betrayed his brother's wife. His own child. Did you know that?"

Nick had no idea Xev had a kid, at all. Still . . .

"I trust him not to harm my mother." Nick didn't know why, just something in the way Xev looked at her said that he would die before he ever allowed any harm to come to her.

Through and through, he believed in Xev.

Tiamat looked less than pleased before she motioned to one of the *zeitjägers*, who quickly left them to obey. "Then it shall be done. And for *your* ally?"

Honestly? He didn't trust *any* of the others at his back. Not even Grim. It just seemed like a bad idea and one step shy of suicide. "Can I pick Simi?"

Tiamat rubbed at her forehead. "You have to pick from your *šarras*."

He'd really rather not. "Kody?"

Chronus glared at him. "Do I have to subtract time from your life sands to get the point across?"

Nick was beginning to not like him.

Truthfully, he didn't want any of them. They weren't his allies. Not really. Grim didn't like him, and that was a major understatement. Laguerre terrified him—she was N-U-T-S, with a cherry on top. Bane . . . was ambivalent to basically everything. Nick didn't know Yrre at all. That only left one, and something in his gut wasn't happy about it, but he had no other choice.

"Livia, then."

Chronus screwed his face up. "Strange you pick the two you've known the least amount of time. Why them?"

Nick shrugged. "I know Grim isn't reliable. Laguerre even less so. I barely know Bane and I've yet to meet Yrre. Xev is the only one I really trust."

Chronus exchanged a puzzled stare with Tiamat. "Then why put Livia at your back?"

"She says I can trust her."

"And that's good enough for you?"

No. Not even a little. But they hadn't really left him with any other choice.

Besides . . .

"If she does me wrong, the shame falls on her shoulders. Not mine. As my mom says—shame comes to those who do shameful things." Nick sighed, dreading what was next, but knowing he couldn't avoid it. "Now, what do I have to do to make them better?"

Tiamat held her hand up and a bright red crow flew to light upon her wrist. She stroked its creepy little head.

"Lerabeth will lead you to the cure you need to awaken your mother and Caleb. You must go to the sacred Nemed in the center of the darkest part of the forest and pick the berries from the largest tree there. Three berries each. Six in total. No more. But be warned, the way is long and fraught with danger. Nothing is as it seems."

"Have you seen the things that attend my high school? I'm kind of used to that."

Tiamat snorted at his humor. "Be careful who you put your trust in, as it could be the last mistake you make. You should also be aware that Noir and Azura are trying to claim bodies for themselves. Should they get to your loved ones first, you will never cure them. Your mother and Caleb will cease to exist. Forever. Therefore, your time is extremely limited. You must beat your brother and the other gods to their mission. Whoever finishes their quest first, wins. The loser dies painfully."

Chronus cleared his throat. "And before you ask. As with life, there are no rules. Nothing is fair. Winner takes all."

Wonderful. Least they could do is let him have a friend or two for the journey. Someone he could put at his back that he actually trusted.

But then maybe that was the point. There were times in life when you had no one at your back but your enemies.

Like his mom so often said, some doors had to be walked through solo.

"So when do I start this disaster?" Nick asked.

Laughing, Tiamat stepped back, and snapped her fingers.

An extremely offended Livia appeared in front of him. Until she saw Chronus and Tiamat.

Her features paled instantly.

With a yelp, she rushed to hide behind Nick so he could protect her from them. Not that he was much more than a flesh wall.

"What is this?" she whispered to him.

"We're getting the cure for my mom and Caleb."

She clutched at him. "What?" she asked in a hushed whisper.

"They"—he jerked his chin toward Chronus and Tiamat—"are giving us the chance to heal them."

Biting her lip, she swallowed hard. "Are you sure we can trust them?"

"Not at all. But it's the only chance they have. So, I'm taking it."

"W-w-w-where are we going?" She'd barely finished asking the question before everything around them went pitch-black nasty. It was so dark, it hurt his eyes and made him see weird spots all around as his eyes struggled to see something out of the absolute nothingness.

When the light unexpectedly returned, Nick flinched in physical pain from it, and found himself in a dark, foggy forest, instead of the streets of New Orleans.

Moonlight cut through spooky trees with knobby knees and hanging moss and thick underbrush and thorns. He'd never seen anything quite like it. Not even Azmodea. Off in the distance, he heard the sound of numerous animals, including wolves. The stench of death, pine, and mistletoe hung heavy around them. It was so pungent, he could taste it.

"What is this place?"

Livia cursed under her breath before she answered him. "Agonia."

"Aga-what?"

"Aga-nee-yah. It's a hell realm, Nick. The one Xev was banished to centuries ago as punishment for betraying his people and killing Caleb's wife."

Oh . . .

Turning around slowly, Nick studied it with care and great curiosity. Other than being dark and a little damp and cold, the place held a strange ethereal beauty to it.

"It doesn't look so bad." Certainly not as horrible

as he'd envisioned it from the way Xev acted about it. He'd expected it to be a blistering desert hell with no comforts at all.

But no sooner had that thought finished than the red crow let out a caw that sounded like a blood-curdling scream. The ground beneath his feet rose up to form a giant beast of a man out of absolutely noth-ing. One with serrated teeth and a massive stone eye in the center of his bulbous head.

An eye he rotated to glare down at them with. "Who are you? Why have you come here?"

Definitely not for a fun-filled Disney vacation.

Nick stepped back cautiously as he decided to take a clue from the one piece of ancient Greek lit he knew, and pulled an Odysseus on the creature. "Nobody."

Unfortunately, Livia must not have ever read *The Odyssey*, as she ratted him out immediately. "You're not Nobody, Nick!" She lifted her chin defiantly toward the giant. "He's the Malachai! You better show him respect or else he'll destroy you where you stand!"

Ah crap. Leave it to her to be honest for once.

And literal.

The giant gaped at them. "Malachai? Here?"

Before Nick could respond with anything more eloquent than a helpless shrug, the entire forest came alive and attacked.

CHAPTER 12

Xevikan became aware of his surroundings with a start. Sensing something was off about the room, he blinked and scowled until he met Kody's equally confused gaze. His whole body was stiff as if he'd been in a fight.

Yet he hadn't.

Had he?

Rolling his shoulders, he tried to make sense of what he felt and saw.

"Where's Nick?" Kody asked him.

Oh yeah, that's what's missing. Nick had been right beside him a moment ago.

"I don't know."

Even Dagon looked baffled by it all.

"What happened?" Rubbing at his temple, Xev felt as if he'd sustained a stunning battle-blow to the head. Nothing had hit him this hard, with this amount of damage, since Caleb. That demon alone could rattle him like this.

Dagon went perfectly still, all of a sudden. "Do you smell *that*?"

"Smell what?" Kody asked.

But Xev knew that unique sickly-sweet stench the moment Dagon mentioned it. "Chronus."

Dagon nodded slowly. "His keepers were here."

Skimming the room as he turned a slow circle, Xev narrowed his gaze on the shadows. "Or still are."

Kody frowned. "I don't understand."

"Neither do I," Dagon breathed.

He met Xev's gaze with eyes that betrayed his own concern that this was quickly escalating into something none of them wanted to live through again. "You think they took Nick for the Source?"

His stomach churned at the very thought of it. And

yet . . . "Why else would the Malachai have vanished? They had to have taken him."

But why?

That was the terrifying question.

If Chronus took possession of Nick, it couldn't be good for anyone. Especially not for anyone in this room. The primal god of order didn't involve himself lightly.

And whenever he did . . .

Tragic things happened for them all.

Xev turned toward Simi. "Charonte? Can you trace the Malachai?"

"The Simi wishes you'd stop calling her that, cursed god. It really, really annoying. She gots a name. Two of them, actually. And they both are quite lovely. So please, pick one and use it when you address me. Otherwise, I might have to do something not so nice to you to get the Simi's point across."

Sighing irritably at him, she closed her eyes and tried to locate Nick.

After a few seconds, she shook her head. "Nope.

The Simi gots no ideas where he went on off to. Maybe he got hungry? Sometimes them boys do that without warning. He the only one the Simi knows who eats as much as she does. He a growing Malachai, after all."

Xev turned around slowly as he studied the symbols on the walls. Symbols that would be useless against Chronus and Tiamat. As well as their pets. He hoped he was wrong. "I have a really bad feeling about this."

Dagon nodded. "As do I. If both Chronus and Tiamat are here, there can only be one reason for it."

"What?" Kody asked.

"Judgment," Xev and Dagon said in unison.

It was the only thing that made sense, and it explained absolutely everything that had happened so far.

The weather. The demons.

Everything.

They should have realized it sooner. But it was so rare a thing that it just hadn't occurred to him that it could be happening, especially since neither he nor Livia had voted or discussed such.

In theory, the šarras should have all met together to decide upon it. *All* of them. Yet none had broached the subject with *him*.

Not even Livia, whom he saw every day.

Kody sucked her breath in sharply. "The others?"

Xev nodded. "They must have called for Nick to be removed as Malachai."

Her jaw went slack as she finally understood the severity of what they might be dealing with. "Has that ever been done before?"

"Only once. Many eons ago. After that . . . there's never been another opportunity. Because of their inherited memories, and tendency and need for vengeance, the Malachais put us down too fast for fear of it happening again. They give us no chance to get together for the vote. And take great pleasure in punishing us for what was done back then."

Dagon turned to Kody. "You better get to Caleb, and make sure Livia hasn't done something to him."

"What do you mean?"

It was Xevikan who answered her question. "If this *is* the Malachai test, she might be working with the others, and there's no telling what she might have done to him to initiate it. It would take four šarras to agree to have a Malachai undergo the hazard. I know I didn't call for it or vote on it. That leaves her, or Bane, as a deciding vote with the others. And I have a feeling Bane didn't bother. Unless he's radically different from the man I remember, he wouldn't involve himself with such politics or treachery."

Kody shook her head. "It doesn't make sense, though. Why would Livia do that after all Caleb and Nick have done to welcome her in?"

Xev laughed bitterly. "It's her nature, Nekoda. If the šarras reached out to her, and asked her to join them, she would have, without hesitation. All she wants is to feel like she's a part of their family. One of *them*."

As Kody started to leave, they heard a knock on the door.

"Menyara?" Dagon asked, thinking it might be her returning with some of their reinforcements.

No one answered from the hallway.

Simi went to the door and peeped through the

hole. "Nope. It that other dog-boy. Zavid . . . Hi, Zavid!" she said in a louder tone as she opened the door for him to enter the condo.

But as he came into the room with an odd swagger and headed straight for the couch where Cherise was still sleeping, they realized this wasn't Zavid.

It was Noir in his body.

Dagon cut his path off to Cherise. "What are you doing here, Father?"

"You know what I want, boy. Now join me or stand aside."

Dagon's gaze went to Xev and Kody. "You asked me earlier to pick a side to die for. I just did."

Stepping back, he let fly a blast from his hands and declared his eternal enmity.

CHAPTER 13

As every single piece of bramble and brush on the forest floor came alive to attack them, Livia shrieked and ran to hide, leaving Nick as the sole nummy treat for them all.

Pissed and aghast, Nick gaped at her as he pulled out his Malachai sword, and expanded its size to fight as best he could. "Livia! A hand, please! You're supposed to be one of my šarras, you know!"

She shrieked and dodged. "I don't fight hand-to-hand. I lead. . . . Other demons fight. Not me. *Never* me. That's not what I do."

Now . . . now *she tells me this? Really?*

Stunned, he gaped at her as he realized just how

badly he'd chosen his partner for this venture. Wow. Talk about hindsight.

And extreme stupidity. Lethal stupidity, for that matter. Bubba would be so proud.

Or disappointed that Nick hadn't paid closer attention in all those survival classes he'd attended and mocked Bubba for teaching. *That'll learn me for daring to make fun of others.*

Artemis was right. Payback was a cat.

Nick fought back as best he could. Alone. "Out of curiosity," he panted, between near-death blows. "Why were you chosen as a šarra, if you can't, and don't, fight?"

She lifted her chin as if offended by what, to him, was an extremely reasonable question. "I'm very handy, I'll have you know! I induce envy and conflict into battle and war."

Oh . . . great. In other words, she was a dung-stirring troublemaker. Pure and simple. That was her entire value in war. Wonderful. Just . . . effing beautiful.

That was exactly what he wanted in a fight right now. Yeah.

Nick cursed himself for not asking that question sooner. That explained why she'd outed him so fast and hurled his bleeding carcass under the bus with the one-eyed giant on their arrival.

That was her nature and her job.

It actually explained a whole lot about many things since he'd brought her on board with his crew. She was a troublemaker. The one who lit the fire in others and watched it burn.

Crap . . . I'm such a flaming moron. And he was about to be a dead one.

He realized too late the mistake he'd made, putting her at his back, and leaving her alone with his friends after he'd freed her.

Oh, the things people learned about others when it was too late to make it better. The last thing anyone wanted on their team was someone whose sole purpose in life was causing drama and stirring up jealousy and intrigue.

How could I have been so stupid? How could he not have seen it before now? Not known what she was doing with her subtle comments and snide innuendo?

But it was easy to do. The thing about jealousy and gossip was that they slipped up on everyone. The trick was to recognize them and stop them immediately. To not let them under your skin.

Because, just like now, they were worthless things that existed for no other purpose than to destroy lives. No one needed them and they served no real use.

Nick looked at Lerabeth. "Hey, bird? A hand or wing here, please?"

The bird snorted. "I'm your guide. Not your soldier. You're on your own, Malachai."

That was how he'd wanted it, but . . . He was beginning to realize alone wasn't all it was cracked up to be, either.

Especially against *this* number of attackers, who were hell-bent on ending his days and ruining his boyish figure.

Sticks and stones continued to rise up from the ground and twist into more armored soldiers. Which would have been cool when he was a kid, playing toy war. But these sticks and stones fully intended to break every bone in his Malachai body and not stop until he was fully dead.

Fine. What do I have in my arsenal?

Lethal sarcasm. A sword. Malfunctioning powers. And one trapped demonic spirit . . .

Nick laughed at a ridiculous idea. A real Hail Mary move.

You are Catholic. Those tend to be your specialties.

True. But there was no guarantee it would work.

You have a full guarantee that it won't work if you don't try it.

Nick ducked as the ugly and very-skilled-with-a-sword giant in front of him swung for his head. He caught the blow with his own sword and parried, then narrowly missed the next attack from another creature moving in at his back. Man, he could use Kody and Caleb, and their wicked sword skills right now. These guys were going to win just by their sheer numbers against him. One person, even a Malachai, couldn't stand for long against this onslaught.

Not alone. Not with his ill-training. Between work and school, he just didn't have the time to focus on martial skills that he needed. *If I live, I swear I'm going to pay more attention to Kyrian, Caleb, and Acheron when they try to teach me this stuff.* No more gaming until he mastered real fighting.

He meant that this time!

"Liv!"

"What?" she snapped irritably. Like *she* had a reason to be snotty when he was the one getting the crap beat out of him? His arm was so bruised right now, he could barely lift it. His back ached. His head hurt. And he wasn't too sure he still had a working spinal cord.

"Help!"

"Can't. They don't have blood for me to drain. That's how I fight."

Well, fan-freaking-tastic. Nick blasted another stone soldier with a bolt of fire and twisted from the grasp of another.

I'm so getting my butt kicked. He couldn't even get to his grimoire to attempt his Hail Mary play.

How had Xev survived it here?

For one thing, he was a god. And a trained soldier, with real battle experience.

And you're the Malachai. You have the power of ancient gods and the Source, too. You can tap the primal powers of the entire universe and blast them to oblivion.

Use the Force, Luke!

All of a sudden, he felt the warmth of his powers building inside him. The fire of it rushed through his blood, faster and faster. His vision darkened. His back burned as his wings began to push through the surface of his skin.

Don't! He heard Nekoda's voice in his head telling him not to morph. *You can't control it!*

She was right and he knew it. He did lose a part of his soul to the darkness every time he accessed those powers he didn't fully understand.

But . . . there were no people here. No one he loved that he could lose or accidentally hurt if he went Malachai.

Yeah, but he had no anchor here either. No one to pull him out of it or calm him down. The gods knew Livia wouldn't do it. She didn't care enough to.

If you don't come back from the Malachai state, your

mom and Caleb will die. As the full Malachai, you won't care about getting them their cure.

If I don't live through this attack, they won't survive either.

There was that. Nick didn't know what to do. He was terrified to use those powers and scared not to, especially since his strength was already starting to fail during the fighting. He wouldn't last much longer in his human body.

Soon, they'd have him.

Maybe this was what Chronus and Tiamat had wanted. A full-blown Malachai. The nightmare beast that didn't care who or what it destroyed. The one that fed on utter misery and destruction.

"Give in to your pain. Not your hatred."

Nick froze at the unexpected deep, masculine voice behind him. That rumbling, thick, lilting brogue would be unintelligible if he wasn't used to taking orders from the Celtic Dark-Hunter Talon. He was the only one who had an accent anywhere near what he'd just heard.

Turning, he saw the shadowed form of a man in the darkness. "Pardon?"

"You want control of your Malachai powers, *boyo*? Give in to the pain and anger. Never the hatred. Set it aside and let it go. Pain will strengthen you and empower you to do better. To be more than what you are. Your hatred will devour you, and swallow you whole if'n you let it. Give in to your pain. Not your bitter hatred."

He made it sound so easy, but it wasn't.

"I'm not sure I know how to do that."

"Then you'll become the Malachai you fear. You might as well let it go, and become him now. No need in getting your arse kicked any worse than what it is. Why endure the misery of it for another minute, eh?"

Nick cursed as one of the beasts kicked him hard in the ribs and another slashed him across the back. He cut one and stumbled away from the next before he sliced a new attacker.

Groaning in pain, he glared at his wise leprechaun tormenter. "Hey, Lucky Charms Legolas? In the meantime, could you hop your butt over here and help a brother out?"

"I wish. Sadly, I lack corporeal form. Like this, I can't even bleed or spit on them."

Livia hissed at the shadow. "Ignore him, Nick. He's just a puck."

"A what?"

"A púca." She spat the term out as if it was the lowest life form ever created. "A will-o'-the-wisp. They're worthless creatures who were damned and cursed by their gods."

"Or a god of war tricked and trapped here by his own kinsmen who stole his powers after he was stupid enough to trust them." The shadow moved closer to the battle. If he was offended by Livia's attack, he gave no clue of it.

Nick groaned as one of the stone creatures hit him hard and sent him to the ground. He tried to rise, but the earth wrapped around his body and held him down. "Do you know how to fight them?" he asked the púca.

"Yes. . . . If I had a real flesh-and-blood body, I could defeat them all."

Grimacing and cursing in pain, Nick locked gazes with him as he had a radical idea. It might be crazy, but it was the only one he could think of. "Will you exchange forms with me long enough to take them out?"

The púca cocked a finely arched brow as if he wasn't quite sure he'd heard those words. "You would trust me?"

"If you give me your word, yes."

The púca pulled back and blinked in utter disbelief. "You'd accept me word?" he asked again.

"Yes."

"Don't do it, Nick! You can't trust a puck! They're liars and thieves. All of them! It's what they do!"

Nick ignored her. "I will trust your honor until *you* give me a reason not to."

The púca hesitated a moment longer before he inclined his head to him. "'Tis a pact then, Malachai, between us brothers. Let me in and I'll ring their blessed bells, till they run weeping home."

Using as little of his Malachai powers as was necessary, Nick swapped his soul with the puck's.

One second, he was on the ground, getting the snot beaten out of him, and in the next, he was the one in the shadows.

Ah, yeah, it felt really good to have a body that wasn't riddled with pain. He could finally draw a deep breath again and not wince or groan from it.

All hail working lungs!

He turned back toward his real body where it was being crushed and bludgeoned by huge, brutish attackers.

Dang, he'd done well to keep them off him. But that was an ugly, ugly sight. And he had no idea how the púca was going to fight them off. For a moment, he fully expected the púca to get them both killed.

Then, with a fierce battle cry and unbelievable dexterity that made a mockery of what Nick could do on a football field, the puck came up from the ground in Nick's body. He swung the Malachai sword and went after the others fast and furious, and with a martial skill Nick envied. A part of him doubted he would ever be that good with a sword.

But then, he wasn't a god of war.

Whoever the púca had been before his banishment, he must have been incredible on a battlefield. 'Cause he still had it. And its evil cousin and all its friends.

In a matter of minutes, the púca had every single attacker scattered and fleeing into the night, begging for mercy and whimpering as they ran.

Yeah, he had rung every bell as promised and found a few in the field no one had seen.

Barely breathing hard, he turned toward Nick and let loose a proud, arrogant smile that said he'd thoroughly enjoyed every second of that brisk fight.

Laying the blade of the sword over his shoulder, he held his hand up before his face and made a tight fist. He kissed it reverently. "I've so missed having a physical body. You just don't know, *boyo* . . . You. Just. Don't. Know."

The anguished joy in his voice concerned Nick greatly. "You are going to give that back, right?"

He met Nick's gaze with a hooded, unfathomable stare. For a second, Nick thought he'd made a bad mistake.

Until the púca held his hand out to him and

grinned in friendship. "Aeron, cursed, damned, and forgotten son of the Morrígan. Nice meeting you, Malachai."

Nick tried to shake his hand, only to see just how frustrating it was to be noncorporeal. No wonder Aeron hated it so.

Gah! It sucked!

Aeron snorted good-naturedly before he exchanged places with Nick again.

Nick took a moment to fully appreciate his "skin" and, best of all, nerve endings, before he faced Aeron's ghost form. The puck's skin was pearly white and translucent. Like shimmering moonlight. His pale eyes reminded him of Acheron's swirling silver ones. Even his hair was silvery white and long. He would be pretty but for the masculine jawline and rugged air that clung to him even though he was a ghostly white. His clothes were those of an ancient warlord, complete with a bare, muscled chest that showed battle scars and a stylized Celtic raven tattoo.

Livia gaped at Aeron. "I can't believe you kept your word to return his body."

Aeron raked a less than pleased stare over her. "To you . . . I wouldn't have." He inclined his head respectfully to Nick. "You trusted me and *that* I would never betray. Trust, much like a woman's love and affection, and brotherly friendship, is a sacred thing, and should never be lightly given nor abused nor taken for granted."

Nick shrank his Malachai sword down and returned it to his pocket. "How long have you been trapped here?"

Aeron shrugged. "Time has long lost all meaning to me. But not to you. Come, *boyo*, and I'll take you to the Nemed."

Nick narrowed his gaze. "How do you know about that?"

A slow, charming grin curved his lips. "I may be weakened, but I do still have some of me powers, and I was just in your body, privy to your thoughts and mission."

Oh, there was that.

Lerabeth finally swooped down to join them. "I am to take him. 'Tis my mission and duty, púca, not yours!"

Nick just loved how she couldn't help with the fight, but could interfere with the help. How typical was that?

Arching an arrogant brow, Aeron stared at the bird. "I know this realm better than anyone." He returned his silvery gaze to Nick. "But you have to keep faith in me, Malachai. If you doubt me at all, for even an instant, I will vanish. Those are the laws of me existence. No matter what happens or what you see, you must continue to believe that I'm leading you to your destination. Do you understand?"

"Got it."

"Then follow me and ignore everything else." He glared meaningfully at the bird. "Especially the barking dogs who are trying to distract you from your goal."

"I'm not a dog, puck."

"I'm not really a púca, bird. I was born the son of the Morrígan and the Dagda."

Bemused by their banter, Nick did have one thing that concerned him about Aeron. "Before we start, can I ask you something?"

"Sure."

"Why are you helping me?"

He glanced away, but not before Nick caught the bitter sadness in his shimmery gaze. "You freed Xevikan when no Malachai ever has. For that kindness, I be owing you."

Nick scowled at the absolute last thing he'd *ever* expected Aeron to say. "How do you know about that?"

"You are the Malachai. Had you drained him and returned him here to this hell to suffer more for that which he didn't do, he'd have immediately come home to me. And that he didn't."

Okay, take that earlier statement back. *That* was the absolute last thing Nick *ever* expected Aeron to say.

His eyes widened in complete and utter shock. "Oh."

Aeron laughed at his gaping expression. "We are brothers and friends, Malachai. Nothing more."

"Ah . . . Gotcha. Whatever you say."

Looking around at the dark forest, Aeron sighed warily. "Here, family and friend are hard to come by. When you are lucky enough to find one, you hold on with both hands and treasure him or her with everything you are. I hope you will appreciate my brother and give him the regard he's due."

"I'm trying. But he doesn't always make it easy."

Aeron laughed. "None of us do, especially when you've been so bloody wounded by everyone around you. Just remember, you owe him your life. Had you not done right by him, I would have left you to them what wanted you today, and let them have their wicked ways with you." He winked at Nick. "No matter what anyone else tells you about Xevikan, he's a good man. A loyal friend. Better than any I know."

"That's what I sense, too."

Aeron inclined his head to him. "Listen to your heart, Malachai. It will never fail you. Other senses lie. Especially the tongues of others. But it never does." He turned into a small bluish-white light that hovered at eye level. "Now, follow me and I'll help you."

Livia curled her lip at Aeron's small, ghostly light form. "He looks like a little fairy."

Aeron snorted. "I am a little fairy in this form, woman. It's what a púca is. If you're trying to insult me masculinity, you'll have to try a lot harder. I was a

Celtic warrior and war god who fought, wrestled, played, and went to war naked with other men, including me brothers and uncles. I'm quite comfortable in me skin and with me life choices, whatever they've been. Excepting the stupidity what led me here. It'll take a lot more than some waspish wisp of a fey shrew calling me names to hurt me feelings, and make me doubt meself."

Nick laughed. "You remind me a lot of a Dark-Hunter I know named Talon of the Morrigantes. Must be a Dark Age Celt thing."

Aeron didn't comment on that.

"This is not the way to the Nemed!" Lerabeth warned as she flew low, next to Nick's shoulder. "Where are you taking us, púca?"

"The shortest route through the cursed woods."

She cawed loudly before she spoke again. "It's a trap, Malachai. You cannot trust him! Púcas are all about deception and lies. Their jobs are to take unwary travelers into the woods and strand them there. It's what they do."

Aeron's light began to dim.

"I'm not doubting you, Aeron." Nick narrowed his gaze at both women. "I have faith in people to do the right thing. It's what my mother taught me. Until I have a reason to, given to me by Aeron himself, I refuse to listen to the evil spewed against him by others. I will trust his actions and my gut instincts, not the words of others who don't know the truth of what lies in his heart."

Aeron hesitated. "You are not a typical Malachai."

"So everyone keeps telling me. Though I'm not sure if it's a compliment or insult the way they say it."

Aeron laughed lightly as he led them through the dense forest.

As they walked onward, Nick considered his earlier fight with the stick and stone people, and the Hail Mary play he hadn't had time to implement. Now that he had breathing room, perhaps it was time to do something he should have done a while ago.

He pulled out his grimoire that was filled with pages where he could consult the spirit that, like Aeron, had been trapped by another's trickery.

Caleb and Kody had told him that there was no

way to free Nashira from the book, but he'd been thinking about that a lot lately, and it seemed to him that if a Malachai had trapped the yōkai, a Malachai should be able to free her.

Just like Nick had done with Xev and Livia. Surely the book was just another type of dimensional prison like this one.

Right?

That made sense to him. If there was a way in, there had to be a way out. Yin to yang. That seemed to be the one definite rule of the universe.

But maybe they were right and he was wrong. There was still so much about being a Malachai he didn't understand. So much about all this that he was absolutely clueless on. Most of the time, he felt like an infant trying to learn to walk.

Unlike the others who'd come before him, he hadn't been raised by a demon mother or demon surrogate who'd instructed him from birth on his true nature. His burgeoning powers had been bound and hidden. Restricted.

He'd been weak and sickly, even for a human child.

Until Ambrose had told him about all this, he'd had no idea of his true birthright. No idea of this hidden world or of any innate preter ability.

He'd only known it existed for less than two years.

Two years. That was it. Until he'd been shot by guys he thought were his friends and saved by Kyrian and given a job, he'd had no idea about Dark-Hunters, Daimons, Were-Hunters, or anything else.

The concept of a Malachai was something he'd never dreamed about in even his most delusional Nintendo-Manga-infested state. It still blew his mind whenever he really thought about it.

So little time to adjust to it all and yet it seemed like eternity in some ways since the day he'd learned the truth. Like he'd always known it was there, somehow.

Maybe it was a form of Malachai instinct that had sensed it was there long before the truth had been revealed. The hidden world just below the surface of the human one. Always lurking in the shadows.

Watching him. Like that creature in the closet that all kids knew was there, yet it vanished whenever a parent opened the door to investigate the darkness.

Yeah, that dude was real, too.

And now that he knew who and what he was, the knowing was so dangerous. Not just for him, but for those he loved and couldn't protect.

Those like his mother, who were still unaware of the truth. It was bad enough for the Kodys and Calebs, who knew. It was so much more for those who had absolutely no clue.

I have to learn to use and control this power. To master it. Not to use it for harm. To use it to keep his family and friends safe from all the ones who would hurt them to get to him.

He'd tried to hide the powers so that his enemies couldn't find him and hurt them, and that hadn't worked.

His only choice was to embrace them. To become what he was born to be.

The Malachai.

There were other creatures born of dark powers

who didn't succumb to them. Creatures who tapped the darkness for good and stayed anchored on the right side without corruption. Acheron. Xev. Caleb. Dagon . . .

"Aeron?"

The puck light paused. "Aye, lad?"

"Do you think you can show me how to control the Malachai within me? You know, like you were trying to tell me, during the fight? All that stuff about using the pain and not the hate? Was that bullcrap or the truth?"

He laughed lightly before he continued on his path through the woods. "It's not control you need to learn."

"How do you mean?"

"The Malachai is never controlled, *boyo*. He's unleashed."

His words only confused Nick more. "But isn't that what we're trying to stop?"

Aeron paused before he took his human form so that he could stand even in height with Nick.

Eye to eye, he met his gaze levelly. "Are you willing to trust me, Malachai? Really trust me? Not just with your life? But with the life of all you hold dear? To lay in me hands the hearts and souls of everyone who matters to you? Mother, lover, brother, family, *and* friend? Think before you answer. Because once you walk this path, there's no way back for you. You'll either be saved . . . or damned for eternity."

CHAPTER 14

Why do you trust Aeron when you shouldn't?"

Nick closed his grimoire as Livia came up to him. They were taking a short break to rest and eat before they renewed their journey into the deepest and most dangerous part of the forest. "Why shouldn't I?"

She scowled at him in disbelief. "You don't know him. At all."

"I know him as well as I know *you*."

Livia snorted disrespectfully. "I'm your Šarru-Ninim."

Yeah, right. Like that made her better, how? He

was supposed to implicitly trust one of the generals whose sole creation was to lead an army of demons to destroy the world.

Sure. Made sense.

Never.

"As chosen by another Malachai. Not me," he gently reminded her.

And still she scoffed at his arguments. "Aeron was so little trusted by his own family that he was banished here to this realm to live out eternity. Doesn't that give you any kind of qualms?"

"No. Not really. Why should it?" Nick gestured to the forest around them. "This is where one of my own generals was banished after his family cursed *him*." He gave her a pointed stare to remind her of how tenuous this argument was. "Do you really want to open that deck, Liv? And have me ask why you were given your position and banished? Trust me. You can't win playing this hand. Think about it."

She pressed her lips together as she fumed. "I can teach you to use your powers, too, you know?"

And every fiber of his being warned him against it. He didn't know why, but he didn't trust her.

Not even a little bit.

"Liv, this isn't a contest. You're not winning or losing. Relax and breathe."

She bristled. "It feels like one. You always make me feel like I'm second place and unimportant. With everyone. Whether it's Kody or Caleb or Zavid. And now Aeron. I feel like you like everyone more than me."

Was she serious? Or insane?

Or just whiney and annoying?

Nick couldn't believe she had all the power she did and he had to placate her damaged ego. For real?

Yet he did. How could she be so needy and insecure? For that matter, how could she be so dense and immature?

He was the teenager. She was thousands of years old. Surely she didn't need him to stroke her ego. Did she?

One look at the expression on her face and it was apparent, she did. How weird was that?

Sighing, Nick shook his head at her. "C'mon, Livia. Some of that can't be helped, and you know it. You are a very attractive woman, and you tend to stand a little too close to me at times."

"Meaning what?"

"Meaning I love Kody, and I don't want her to get the wrong idea about *us*. Nor do I want her feelings hurt. And not that I ever would, but I could sit naked on top of Caleb's lap all day long, and spoon him in bed, and eat from his spork at school while he hand-fed and burped me, and she wouldn't care. *You* sit next to me while she's across the table, and it's open war."

"That's not fair."

"Fair or not, it's how feelings work. I wouldn't care if she sipped on a single straw with Brynna during lunch or licked chocolate sauce from between Brynna's fingertips . . . or shared a single shower stall with her and LaShonda after PE class—in fact, I've had that fantasy a few times. But if Kody ever held hands with Caleb or kissed his cheek, I'd go Liu-Kang-*Mortal-Kombat all* over his giant, hairy ass."

He narrowed his gaze on her. "As the queen of

jealousy, you are well aware of how this works, so don't play all innocent with me like you don't know."

"She should trust you."

Yeah, right. "This isn't a matter of trust and you know that. It's a matter of respect. Kody trusts me and I trust her because we respect each other's feelings when we're together and apart, and we don't play those games with each other's emotions. I don't try to make her jealous and she doesn't do that to me. We don't have to. So I'm sorry that you feel like you're second place, but you're not my girlfriend and you're a little handsy with my body's no-zones whenever you're near me, so I do, and will *always,* maintain three car lengths' distance between us at all times."

And then she did what she always did whenever she was near him. She walked into his personal space and put her hand on his chest before she trailed her hand lower. "You and I could have a good time together, Nick. If you'd let us."

He pulled her hand away as it neared the waistband of his jeans. "I don't think of you like *that*."

"You could."

And that was the problem. "Yeah, and I don't want to be *that* guy. It's just a short jump from that to wearing obscene Mardi Gras beads and hanging out on Bourbon Street and sexually harassing women who'd rather switch teams than look at me. No offense, I don't want to be the poster boy for why women should consider swearing off men altogether, for eternity. I'd rather be a stand-up guy who speaks well for my gender rather than a two-timing mandork."

She scoffed at him and raked a sneer over his body that would have shriveled the gender of anyone who possessed lesser conviction. "You are a Malachai! Why don't you ever act like one!" She shoved him. Hard.

Furious at her unwarranted attack, Nick tripped and hit the ground.

Livia unleashed her wings and took her demon form. Her breathing ragged, she stood over his body, glaring down at him. "You're pathetic! Weak! Disgusting! You have all the power of the universe to take what you want and you never use it! What is wrong with you?"

In that moment, he fully understood what Aeron had tried to teach him earlier.

The difference between hatred and pain.

This was the pain Aeron had talked about. The anguish Nick had felt all his life of being worthless and despised, and of feeling like nothing. That desire not to lash out and hurt others in his hatred, but to prove them wrong whenever they'd judged him for things he couldn't help. To show them that he wasn't poor gutter trash to be thrown away. That he wasn't invisible. That he was a human being with human feelings.

That he mattered.

This wasn't hatred in his heart.

It was bitter shame.

And it burned like a hungry fire in his gut. Throwing his head back, he let the fury of it roll out of him in a fierce, deep roar. One that echoed through the forest and caused animals to take flight and flee in stark terror.

His wings shot out as his body instantly transformed to its true Malachai nature. Stronger and deadlier than ever.

The color faded from Livia's face as she backed away obsequiously. She bowed low before him as she begged and pleaded for his forgiveness.

From the darkness around them, Aeron came forward with an arch stare. He wasn't afraid of Nick, only cautious. "Are you in control, *boyo*?"

Nick looked around the forest with his intense sight that not only saw, but *felt* the very air around him. For the first time ever, he was himself in his Malachai's body. There was no rage beast wanting to consume and devour everything within reach. No desire to kill or to maim.

He was human *and* beast.

Only more powerful.

Fully in control. United. A single creature that understood both sides of its furious nature. The brutal and the compassion.

Stunned to silence, Nick allowed the enormity of the moment to wash over him. Could it be? He held his hand up to see the marbled black and red flesh. The clawed hands.

Yeah, he was definitely and fully demoned out.

"Nick?" Aeron tried again. "Can you understand me?"

"Yeah. I feel normal. But weird. Really, really weird." He sounded even weirder. It was the first time he'd been able to really converse with someone as a demon.

Laughing, Aeron winked at him. "You found it, eh?"

Nick nodded slowly. "I think I get it, though. Why you said it could endanger everyone I loved." He shifted back to his human body and brushed his hand through his hair. "Yeah, definitely, don't try this at home, kids. Only with professional drivers, on a closed track."

A slow, knowing smile spread across Aeron's face. "But try it again? Just to be sure?"

Nick did.

And again, it worked. For the first time, he had complete control over his body and his powers. "Have I mastered it?"

Aeron wasn't so quick to agree. "You're getting there. No doubt. It'll still take more practice."

He offered Nick a proud smile. "Just remember,

your temper will always be the key to unlock those powers, and you'll have to ride herd on that temper for all your days. As the Malachai, hatred will forever be your weakness. Your undoing. That special place where you'll want to go for comfort. But it's the one place you must avoid at all costs, less you want to eat your neighbors and family."

"Yeah . . . no. Think I'll pass."

"Wise choice, lad."

Livia straightened and watched him with a peculiar light in her eyes. One Nick wasn't quite sure about. But he didn't have time to worry over that. Let her have her tantrum later. Honestly, he was tired of dealing with her and her theatrics. The more he was around her, the more grateful he was for Kody, who never brought drama to his door—other than the demons who followed her there that she couldn't elude. Yet that wasn't her fault. She always did her best to get rid of them first.

Right now, he had to save his mom and Caleb. For all he knew, his unknown, mysterious half-brother was nearing the end of *his* test.

And Nick had to beat him to it. While he honestly would be glad to hand over the reins of Malachai to someone else, *anyone* else for that matter, he couldn't allow his mother to stay asleep.

They had to get the berries to wake her. That was his goal.

Nick launched his wings, but kept his human body. Ah yeah, now this was cool. "So . . . shall we fly to the Nemed?"

With a nod of approval, Aeron turned into the ball of ghost light, and led him through the forest with Lerabeth and Livia trailing behind them.

Now that Nick was able to access his Malachai powers without them taking him over, they were able to reach the tree in a matter of minutes.

Nick also realized that his mission had been a manufactured trick by Chronus and Tiamat. The tree was so tall that without his Malachai wings, he wouldn't have been able to reach the berries at all. They hung too high. But there was also another problem.

He frowned up at the fruit that was nestled along

the leaf-filled branches. "Do I pick the black, green, or red berries?"

"Blackberries," Livia answered.

"Nae!" Aeron shouted as Nick reached for them. "Nemed blackberries are for death. The green are unripened fruit. The red are what you be needing to revive your loved ones, *boyo*."

Livia scoffed at him. "He's lying to you, Nick. For once, listen to *me*!"

Nick growled low in his throat, tired of Livia's eternal bickering and whining. "Lerabeth? Which is it?"

"I was to lead. You're here. You pick the berries you were told."

There was only one problem with that. "No one said anything about color-coded berries, crow woman. They just said to pick six."

"Then pick six and be done with it."

Nick wanted to wring the neck of that unhelpful red crow. He glanced to Livia, who was glaring at him as if she could kill him herself.

She might be one of his generals, but every part of him said that he should listen to Aeron. "Fine. Then

I'm going with the one who calls this place home. If anyone should know which to pick, Aeron should be he."

He reached for the red ones.

The moment Nick had all six in his hand, Lerabeth opened the portal back to their world.

Nick hesitated. "Can Aeron return with us?"

"I brought two in and was only told to take two out. That is all I can do."

Nick scowled as he faced the one person he owed everything to. Without the púca they'd have never made it. It didn't seem right to leave him here and go home after everything Aeron had done for him.

"Aeron—"

"It's fine, *boyo*." He gave Nick a cheerful smile that didn't quite reach his pale eyes. "Give Xev me best."

Nick nodded glumly, feeling like crap over this. It wasn't fair or right.

But then, life seldom was.

As Nick started to turn to leave through the portal, Livia ran up to him and grabbed his Malachai dagger from his back pocket. Before he could ask her what she was doing with it, she cut his throat and vanished through the portal, then sealed it closed.

Stunned by the pain, Nick fell to his knees as he tried to stop the bleeding with his own hands. But it was useless. He was going to die.

He couldn't believe what had just happened.

Livia had murdered him.

After everything he'd done for her.

I saved her life. Kept her from having to go back to her prison.

And this was how she repaid him. Kyrian was right. *No good deed goes unpunished.*

Kneeling by his side, Aeron cawed and summoned a small murder of crows to them. Since he couldn't hold or grasp anything, he had the crows bring straw and brush to make a pillow for Nick's head. "Breathe, Malachai, stay calm."

Easier said than done. His senses reeled as his fury mounted over her actions. Livia had betrayed him in the worst sort of way.

The bitch had cut his throat! Literally. And left him to die alone in this realm without friend or family!

But there was nothing to be done about it. In a few minutes, he'd bleed out and be gone from this life.

Forever.

And in that one heartbeat when his anger and hatred were at their highest point, when all he wanted was vengeance and blood, he let it go and released all that negativity from his body and heart.

There was no need in holding on to it now at the very end of his life. Not when he had so many regrets that saddened him and made him wish he'd spent his finite time more productively.

And with the people who'd mattered most to him.

The biggest regret inside his heart was his inability to save his mother and Caleb.

Not being with Kody, during these final precious minutes.

Yet there was one last regret he could take care of before he died. While it wouldn't render aid to those closest to him, it would to one who had helped them all in the past.

At least he hoped it would. And if he could help one last person before he died, then he could go in peace.

His eyesight blurring and fading, he pulled out his grimoire. It and the dagger Livia had stolen were two of the most powerful tools a Malachai had, and the two he'd first mastered. Sort of. No one ever really mastered the grimoire since it was possessed by an ancient *yōkai*—a mischievous eastern oracle spirit that had been trapped by his father and tricked into the book. The only way to communicate with her was to offer Nashira a blood sacrifice.

Blood has power and yours has more than most. Make sure you guard it and bleed as little as possible. Caleb's words of warning went through his head.

A little late since he was now bleeding all over the place. It saturated his ugly Hawaiian shirt and the ground around him. And it covered the necravitacon where his father had trapped her centuries ago.

"Nashira," Nick gasped weakly, hoping this worked and that he could free her before he died, "hear me and step forward. Not in words, this time, but in your woman's form. The time has come for you to be restored. A favor to a favor. A Malachai once took you from this world, now the time . . . has come . . . for a

Malachai to return you." He held the book to his chest and prayed for it to work.

The air whipped around him, like a violent hurricane. Strong and furious. It drove the crows back as a cloud of dark purple smoke rolled out of the grimoire. It rose up into a column by Nick and Aeron's side.

A pair of perfect lavender eyes formed to stare incredulously at him. The smoke turned into tendrils of long white hair that was fastened with purple flowers bound in flowering ribbons. Then, ever so slowly, the smoke solidified into the rest of her body.

The white crow tengu that his father had captured centuries ago and bound to his service against her will was a lot tinier than Nick had imagined her. More fragile in appearance . . . especially given her nasty and biting sarcasm. But in reality, she was similar to a tiny, adorable pixie. Like Simi in her real form, she had pointed ears and a pointy chin.

She was so beautiful. In a unique, impish way. How he wished he'd been able to free her in the human realm and not here. But maybe she'd be able to cross over again. Someday.

And at least she again was in her own body.

Gaping in disbelief, she stared down at her hands and turned them back and forth before she met Nick's gaze. "I'm restored?"

Nick nodded and offered her a smile even as the darkness stole his sight. "With my dying breath, I free you from your slavery. I'm just sorry it took me so long to figure out how to do it."

CHAPTER 15

Nick came awake slowly as he remembered Livia's vicious attack on him in Agonia. And he knew he was dead.

Because I'm an idiot.

He'd been looking for treachery to come at him from everyone *but* the one who'd actually done it. Xev. Dagon. Acheron. Ambrose. Caleb. Aeron. Lerabeth. Even Kody and Menyara.

Yet it had been the one he hadn't been paying attention to who'd done it.

Yeah, ain't this a bitch? Never failed. Never came from the bus you saw, that was blowing the horn and flashing its lights. It was always that sneaky SOB in a small Toyota coming up behind you that you missed.

Nick swallowed, wishing things were different. But he knew better. There was no way to have suffered such a vicious neck wound and not feel pain from it.

Not without death.

And he'd never felt better than he did right now.

Nothing hurt.

He bit his lip, scared to open his eyes and find out where he'd ended up for eternity. He was hoping he'd gone north to a pearly gate where Peter would be waiting with a lengthy list of all the things he'd screwed up in his life, but as the Malachai, he wasn't betting on it.

Please don't let it be really hot here. New Orleans in August was about as hot as he wanted to deal with. And he definitely didn't want to smell rotten eggs for eternity. He'd had enough of Kyrian's dirty laundry for that.

And Bourbon Street alleyways after Mardi Gras.

"Nick?" A soft, gentle hand stroked his cheek. One that didn't belong to Kody or his mother.

Confused, he opened his eyes to find Nashira there. "Am I dead?"

A slow smile spread across her beautiful, fragile features. "No. We saved you."

"We?"

She inclined her head to the other side of the room.

Nick shifted to see . . . holy crap. It was Aeron. Only he wasn't a puck anymore. He was now fully restored, too.

How had that happened?

No longer pale-skinned, Aeron had a glowing, tawny complexion. And he was a tall beast, too. Close to Acheron's massive butt-kicking height. Or maybe he just seemed that tall given his tough aura and that deadly, piercing expression on his face.

"What happened to *you*?"

A slow blush crept over Aeron's skin that mottled his cheeks and tempered his badass aura. He shifted slightly in his chair. "Remember what I told you about holding your temper, Malachai?"

"Yeah?"

"Hold your temper."

A bad feeling went through Nick. "Why are you telling me that?"

Rising to his feet, Aeron put a little more distance between them. Enough that he could bolt if he had to.

Ah, that can't be good . . .

Nick's scowl deepened that someone as powerful and deadly as Aeron would ever be so skittish around him. Honestly? He doubted he could touch him on skill.

And given his current condition, he knew he couldn't catch him. So then, what was the deal?

"In order to save your life, I had to take a small involuntary blood donation from you."

Nick froze as those words rattled around his three brain cells. "You drank my blood?"

"Aye."

He screwed his face up at the mere thought of it. "Dude, that's so gross. I hope you brushed your teeth afterward. Saw a dentist. Drank a gallon of Listerine."

Aeron laughed.

"I told you he wouldn't be angry for it." Nashira

took Nick's hand and held it in both of hers before she bowed low to him. "I can't believe that you were dying and your last act was to think to free me."

"Well, I just figured out how to do it. But I wasn't completely sure it would work. I wanted to ask Caleb about it, then he got sick before I could. And all this other crap happened. Since I was dying, I figured it was worth a shot before I went. No need in you being trapped in there for the rest of eternity if you could go free."

Tears filled her lavender eyes as she squeezed his hand. "And that is why we worked together to save your life. Why we have watched over you and worried that you wouldn't pull through."

Touched by her concern, Nick wasn't sure what to say to that.

Aeron came forward finally and handed Nick a small, folded handkerchief.

Nick opened it to find the berries he'd picked for his mother and Caleb. "Ah man, this is great, but how do we open the portal now that Lerabeth is gone?"

Aeron shrugged nonchalantly. "It's not a problem. You're the Malachai. At **11:34**, the veils weaken. It's easy for you to open a portal and go through."

"**11:34**? Why then?"

"Invert it and turn it over."

Nick blinked at Aeron. "I'm an idiot with a head injury. Want to help a brother out and make it easy on me?"

Nashira snorted. "Take it from me, our Malachai isn't big on riddles or puzzles. He doesn't even like to play Zelda."

"Yeah. Attention span of a gnat. ADD."

Aeron sighed heavily. "It's a numeric cipher for 'hell.' Before it came to mean 'infernal damnation,' it was simply a word that meant 'hidden behind a veil' or 'to keep hidden.' Even the term 'hell-mouth' is an ancient one that was used by my people long before missionaries came to our shores."

Nashira nodded. "Whenever it turns **11:34** over a hell-mouth or near a hell-gate, the veil thins enough for something to punch its way through from one realm to another. There's always a chance something can come through. It's why you saw so many *zeitjägers* earlier. The atmospheric unrest put all the guardians on notice that the portals were about to be accessed."

Aeron crossed his arms over his chest. "Even I knew from here that Noir was trying to cross from Azmodea into the human realm."

"Did he make it?"

Nashira hesitated before she answered his question. "I'm sorry, Nick. They weren't able to stop him."

Fear and dread tangled inside him. If Noir had made it through, then he'd gone after those nearest and dearest to Nick. And most likely, Livia was hoovering up to Noir, right now.

Playtime was over.

Ignoring the pain, Nick rose slowly to his feet. "What do I need to do to get us through?"

Aeron snorted disdainfully. "You're the Malachai. Transform to your body. Conjure a portal. Punch through it."

Gah, he made it sound *so* easy.

Nashira put her hand on Nick's shoulder. "But don't be hatin' when you do it."

Nick laughed at her reminder. "Where are all the riddles and rhymes you were so quick to torment me with in the past?"

She smiled at him. "I'm no longer locked in the necravitacon. My desire to make you crazy with them is gone now." She rose up to kiss his cheek. "My only desire is to help you and to thank you for my freedom."

"You're welcome." Nick rolled his shoulders and shook his hands to loosen them. "All right. Let's try this."

Aeron moved to stand by his side so that he could help guide him through it.

With a deep breath for courage, Nick tapped his powers and let the strength of the Malachai run through him.

For a moment, as he remembered what Livia had done, he felt himself slipping toward the beastly side of it and losing control.

But he pulled himself back by sheer force of will. Livia wasn't worth the cost of losing his future. Of losing Nekoda and his mother. *They* were the prize.

Hoping Aeron and Nashira weren't setting him up

like Livia had, Nick did what they said and punched a hole from Agonia back into the mortal realm he called home.

For a full terrifying minute—the longest one of his life—he didn't think he could do it. But after a few more nerve-wrecking seconds, he finally made the hole through.

He allowed Nashira and Aeron to cross over first, and then he followed through and closed the portal.

"Where are we?" Aeron asked in a low whisper as he glanced about at the bed and dresser.

"My room." Nick kept his tone barely audible. Just in case.

Using his telepathy, he reached out to Kody to see where everyone was.

She didn't respond.

His panic set in. They should all be here, in his house, where it was safe and protected.

Why weren't they here?

Nashira touched his arm to anchor him. "Breathe, Malachai. Don't panic. Don't get angry. Not until you have more information."

Grateful for her presence, he closed his eyes and used his powers to search the condo.

It *was* empty.

Rage tore him apart as he saw the blood and fighting in afterimages that had been recorded by Menyara's spells. Noir had been here and he'd attacked them all.

"Nick . . . Calm yourself."

Honestly? He didn't want to be calm. He wanted Noir's throat. The Malachai in him was a fierce, demanding beast.

And right now, it was hungry. Bloodthirsty. It craved the throats and hearts of his enemies.

Of anyone who'd ever done him harm.

His breathing ragged as he struggled for control, he opened his eyes to stare at Aeron. "Is this how the world looks to you, too?"

"Do you know what my name means?"

Nick shook his head.

"Carnage and slaughter. Back in the time when the Dagda and the Mórrígan ruled, there were altars set for me throughout the kingdoms where we were worshiped. The day before a battle was to be fought, three strong warriors—two men and one female, in the prime of their youth—would be sacrificed to me to ensure me favor for their cause and their victory."

"And I should take what from all that?"

"That it was never the blood of me own that I hungered for. It's the throats of me enemies I crave. Their blood that nourishes me hunger and makes me want to feel it washing over me skin and bones, until I'm drunk from it. So, aye. I understand what you see and feel. That need you have to rip them apart and relish every cry they scream for mercy and death."

Nick took a step to the left.

Aeron wrapped his fist in Nick's shirt and pulled him closer as those pale eyes showed every ounce of furious horror that lived inside the ancient being. "But as a fellow brother in the deathly arts, I'm telling you now, *boyo*, don't give in to that hatred. Remember what I told you. Save yourself while you're able. Don't lose your soul for vengeance. Think of your Nekoda and let her pull you back from your violent ways, and if there's killing to be done, let me have it. I'm already damned and lost. There's still hope for you, lad."

Aeron released him and stepped back. He clapped a hand against Nick's cheek. "Better?"

Not quite sure, but definitely intimidated by the war-god, Nick nodded and took a second to get ahold of his emotions.

Finally, he had enough control to use Menyara's spells to see what had happened and to let it play out. Yes, his anger wanted control, but he kept a tight leash on it and refused to give in to it.

He would *not* be his father.

I am the Ambrose Malachai. And he would walk his own path. Right or wrong.

With a deep, fortifying breath, he looked at Aeron, then Nashira. "They're at Caleb's."

And they were under one bloody, bad attack.

CHAPTER 16

W e can't hold them! They're busting through!" Kody shouted a warning to Simi, who was holed up in Caleb's bedroom with his body and Cherise's.

Demons, crows, insects—you name it, Noir was throwing it at them.

Kody hadn't seen anything like this since she'd been in battle against Ambrose, centuries from now. They were losing, and she was terrified.

After Noir had taken possession of Zavid, Dagon had bought them enough time to gather Cherise and retreat with her here, out of his reach.

But that hadn't lasted long.

Noir had found them. Now they were fighting again.

Suddenly, a bright flash lit the foyer below. Livia appeared in her demon form. Holding her head high, she surveyed the combatants smugly.

"Give up, Nekoda!" she shrieked from the bottom of the stairs. "Nick is dead. I'm the new Malachai!" She held his sword above her head as proof of her bold declaration.

From the balcony above, Nekoda froze as those words hit her like a fist to her heart. No! It wasn't true. It couldn't be true!

Tears choked and blinded her as she nocked another arrow on her mother's bow. "You lie! I don't believe you! You're not powerful enough to take down Nick." Kody let fly the arrow at Livia's head.

She ducked and sent a blast toward her.

It missed and shattered the window over Kody's head. "Whose blood do you think covers me?" Livia asked. "I cut his throat with his own sword!"

Even though Livia had the Malachai sword, Kody refused to believe Nick was dead. She'd feel it if he was gone.

It was a trick.

"You lie!!" she growled. Nick knew better than to die on her. She'd never forgive him for that.

Never!

The entire house shook as Noir and Thorn and Menyara went at each other outside.

Kody was about to run out of ammunition. Beleaguered and exhausted, she hadn't been this tired since she'd fought against Nick beside her brother. Lightning flashed. Rain poured and demonic screams echoed all around.

Still, she fought on. It was what her parents had taught her to do. Past the pain. Past the exhaustion.

Never give up. Never give in.

Livia rose with the sword. "All of you!" she screamed violently. "Listen to me! You have to obey me now! *I* am the Malachai! I have his power! I took his blood and his sword!"

As those shrill words carried, the fighting slowly came to a stop.

Even Noir.

Covered in blood, he returned to the room to stand by Livia's side. "What is this?"

She held the sword out for his inspection. "I used the Malachai's sword to cut his throat and take his power. I am the leader of the ušumgallu! Hear me, Chronus and Tiamat. God of order and goddess of chaos. I am now your lead servant. The one who will oversee the final battle."

Menyara and Thorn appeared next to Kody's side on the balcony, as did a wounded Xev and Dagon.

"What madness is this?" Xev growled.

Tears filled Menyara's eyes. "It's not possible. Not my Nicky."

Tiamat appeared before Livia and held her hand out. "Let me see the sword."

Tucking her wings in, Livia handed it over.

The goddess examined it before she nodded. "It is indeed the Malachai's sword, and it bears the blood of Ambrose."

Unable to breathe and choking on her sobs, Kody fell to her knees as she heard those words of bitter confirmation. Her only solace was that Cherise wasn't awake to hear them, too. It would kill her to know that Nick was dead.

Xev picked her up and cradled her against his chest, but there was nothing that could comfort her while she hurt like this. Nothing other than Livia's throat.

Her mind set on vengeance, Kody pushed herself away from him and started forward.

But Xev caught her in his arms. "Don't you dare. They'll kill you."

"Let them! He's all I have." Sobs racked her entire body as pain and grief permeated every molecule of her being. Her heart felt as if it'd been ripped out. She couldn't lose anyone else. She was tired of burying those she loved. Tired of saying good-bye.

Tiamat handed the sword back to Livia. "Pick your generals, Malachai."

Grim and Laguerre stepped forward with cocky grins.

Livia walked past them both.

Just as she was about to pick random demons, a deep, Cajun drawl rang out in the room.

"Oh no, you din't! Put my sword down. You getting bitch-cooties all over it. Don't know if I'll ever be able to sandblast them off that handle, you skank."

Kody's breath caught in her throat. Her gaze blurred by tears, she scanned the crowd until she saw the tall, proud, black-and-red-skinned, winged Malachai.

Ambrose!

Oh, she should hate that body with every last bit of her soul. But right then . . .

She wanted to kiss him.

"Nick," she breathed as relief coursed through her veins.

He flew into the room with two others she didn't recognize. But by the way Xev stiffened, it was obvious he knew at least one of them.

Livia turned on Nick with a shriek. "No! I killed you! You're dead! I saw it."

Nick scoffed in that arrogant way only he could. "Obviously not. Really, we need to talk about your aim. Good thing you're not a man. 'Cause they'd ban you from restrooms all over town. Run you out on rails."

When she went to attack, Nick threw his arm out and yanked his sword from her grasp. Then he pinned her to the wall with his powers, and faced Tiamat.

Nick was in no mood to play with the ancient goddess. While he was well aware of the fact that she could splinter him to pieces, he really didn't care. "I'm assuming I passed your test?"

All she did was nod.

"Good. Does this mean *I* get to pick my generals now?"

Again, she nodded.

Nick's gaze never left hers as he rattled off his list with ease. "Nashira. Xev. Dagon. Aeron. Kody. Caleb."

"You can't do that!" Grim and Laguerre protested in unison.

Tiamat quirked her lips. "Actually, he can choose whomever he wishes to lead his armies. That is his prerogative." She turned back toward Nick. "But be warned with that lineup, Malachai, you have chosen one of the most powerful groups ever assembled. Together, they could wield enough power to one day kill you."

Nick inclined his head to her. "I'm counting on it."

Tiamat and Chronus closed ranks around Noir. "Time for you to return to your realm."

"No!" he snarled. "That wasn't the deal."

Chronus shrugged. "The balance is maintained and Ambrose has proven himself worthy of his bloodline. He bested his competition. Passed every test and resurrected himself. He's even subdued his old generals and chosen new ones. Order is restored and he's claimed his birthright."

Tiamat wrinkled her nose. "Deal with it."

Noir's hate-filled gaze went straight to Nick. "I know who you are now, boy. This is only the beginning."

Nick crossed his arms over his chest and lifted his chin with every bit of stubborn Cajun pride he possessed. "You might know my name and face, but you know nothing about me *personally*. And that's your mistake. If you did, you'd know not to threaten me or mine." He raked a sneer over Noir's body. "If you think you can take me, you better not come alone." He cast his gaze around at the bodies on the floor. "And don't forget to stock up on body bags before you do."

With a furious growl, Noir vanished and took a screaming Livia with him.

Grim exchanged a furious glower with Laguerre before he closed the distance between him and Nick. In full reaper mode, he stood toe-to-toe with Nick's Malachai form. "This little slight here today will not be forgotten, boy. So let me put Noir's sentiments into words you and your little demonteers can fully understand . . ." He swept his gaze around to each of them. "Consider yourselves served. It's on, bitches."

With a snap of his bony fingers, he, Laguerre, Pain and Suffering all vanished from the room.

"On what?" Dagon asked.

Snorting, Kody explained while Nick looked around for Zavid.

Menyara gave a sad shake of her head. "Zavid's gone, Nick. I'm sorry. Livia sacrificed him to bring Noir over to this realm."

"No . . ." Nick couldn't believe it as pain for his friend racked him. "What about Caleb?"

"He's upstairs, still unconscious. She tried with him, but he was too powerful. Even asleep, he fought her."

Thank God for that.

"My mom?"

Kody approached him slowly. "She's with Caleb, and Simi's guarding them both."

Breathing in relief and grateful beyond measure to his friends, he finally transformed back into his human body.

Now that he no longer looked like the creature who'd coldly murdered her and her brother, Kody brushed her hand through his hair. "Should I ask about the new Malachai you?"

He gave her a sheepish grin before he pulled her into his arms and buried his face in her neck so that he could inhale that sweet vanilla scent that always made his head spin. "I found a way to control it. At least for now."

She held him close. "I hope you know what you're doing."

"Never," he snorted, then kissed her.

Thorn sauntered over to Nick and let out a weary breath as he eyed him. "I hope to God you know what you're doing with this new group you've chosen, kid."

By the way he stared at Aeron, Nick had a feeling there was some serious history between them. But neither gave a clue as to what it was.

Same with Thorn and Dagon.

Holding tight to Kody, Nick shrugged at Thorn's warning. "At least I know something about these šarras and their loyalties."

Thorn snorted. "Familiarity breeds contempt." And with that warning, he left them alone.

Nick watched as Xev stared at Aeron in utter disbelief. He circled around him as if he was afraid to touch him.

"You're corporeal? How?"

"I borrowed a little blood." Aeron cast a sheepish gaze toward Nick.

Xev gaped. "He didn't kill you for it?"

"Not yet."

Shaking his head, Xev held his hand out to Aeron,

who hesitated before he took it. Xev pulled him in for a man hug. "Thank you, little brother."

Aeron nodded.

Xev kissed him lightly on the head before he released him. He stepped back and met Nick's curious stare. "I owe him my life in ways you can't even begin to imagine."

Nick held his hands up in surrender. "Hey, I don't judge. My own life's too screwed up for that. To each, his own."

As everything slowly returned to normal, Nick and Kody went upstairs with Aeron and Xev to give the berries to his mom and Caleb and return them to normal.

"Are you sure this is going to work?" Nick asked as they carefully dispensed the berries' juices.

Aeron gave him a droll stare. "You're not seriously asking that, are you?"

He'd barely finished speaking before Caleb woke up, choking and gasping. The minute he saw them in his room, he cursed Xev. "What's he doing in my house?"

Xev sighed heavily. "Nice to have you back, brother." He vanished a minute later.

Nick let out a tired breath. "You know, he saved your life today."

Caleb glared at him and scoffed. "No, Nick. He took my life when he allowed my enemies to have my wife's. And I wish to the gods that you'd never allowed him to go free."

"Is that why you're trying to bargain for your freedom?"

Caleb scowled at him. "What new paint fumes have you been inhaling?"

"Livia told me that you'd been summoning stronger powers in an effort to break free of me, for a while now."

Caleb pressed his hand to his head as if he had a severe migraine. "What? Are you totally stupid? Wait. It's you. I know that answer."

He let out a slow breath before he spoke again. "Look, dumbass . . . I don't care what stupidity Livia has filled your head with. The only person who could possibly free me from you, outside of a grisly death and damnation I'd rather not face, is my father. And I wouldn't trust him for anything. Not that he would do it anyway since he's currently Noir's right hand. To get free of you, I'm rather sure he'd require I unleash you on the world, which would defeat the purpose of being free of you. So no, I haven't been trying to get free of you as there is no point in it." Caleb scratched at his face. "Besides, I'm getting way too attached to your annoying stupidity. You're like a pet that chews up my favorite shoes."

He should probably be offended by that, but coming from Caleb's surly hide, that was a deep avowal of love.

"I'm glad you're not dead. Today." Nick left the room only to hear Caleb's shout about why and how Dagon was there.

Ignoring him and leaving it for Menyara to explain, Nick joined Simi in the guest room and waited with bated breath until his mom opened her blue eyes.

She scowled up at him before she slowly glanced around the room. "Where am I? How did I get here?"

"Don't you remember, Ma?"

"Um . . . no."

"Our power went out. We came over to Caleb's. You were on the stairs when the storm broke the window and some of it hit you. You fell." Nick committed that lie to memory so that he could confess it to the priest on Saturday. Of course, he had a lot to talk to the priest about. Most of which left Father Jeffrey thinking he was writing a novel.

But that was okay by him.

He was just grateful that he was alive and that his mother was still with him.

Which reminded him of one more extremely important thing he had left to do.

EPILOGUE

N ick, Simi, Kody, and Dagon stood deep in the bowels of Tartarus, where Simi's "scary" room was located. She was right. It was kind of slimy where they kept the Eye of Ananke.

But for once, they'd had an easy time getting to it, since their guide was the son of the goddess Hekate.

Turns out, if you're friends with a friend of Hades and your mom is best friends and the handmaiden of Persephone, you're gold to visit his realm. All Hekate had demanded was a kiss and hug from her son.

Simi picked up the dark green gem and handed it to Nick. "Oooo sparkly. So what's this for, anyway?"

"Not real sure."

Dagon took it out of Nick's hands and pressed it to Nick's forehead. "It functions like a third eye. You place it there and you can see the future."

Nick fell silent as he saw not just the future, he saw *all* of them. It was like being in the alternate universe all over again.

Only this time, he saw every universe, including this one.

Now he understood exactly what Ambrose had been talking about.

No wonder his future self had been so freaked out by everything.

There before him, he saw clearly every single mistake each of them would make that would bring them closer to the end of the world.

It was horrifying.

But the one question still remained . . .

Could it be stopped before it was too late?

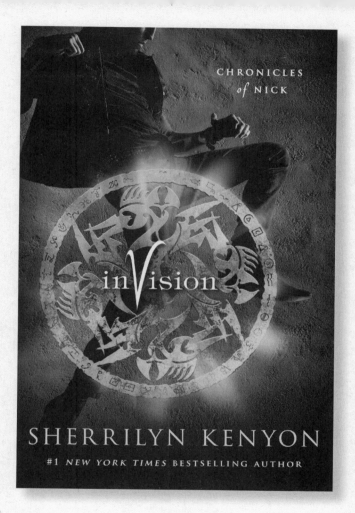